blue
rider
press

BIG LAW

BIG LAW

RON LIEBMAN

BLUE RIDER PRESS

NEW YORK

blue
rider
press

An imprint of Penguin Random House LLC
375 Hudson Street
New York, New York 10014

Library of Congress Cataloging-in-Publication Data

Names: Liebman, Ronald S., author.
Title: Big law / Ron Liebman.
Description: New York : Blue Rider Press, 2017.
Identifiers: LCCN 2016026671 | ISBN 9781101982990 (hardback)
Subjects:
LCSH: Lawyers—New York (State)—New York—Fiction. |
Corporations—New York (State)—New York—Fiction. |
Corruption—New York (State)—New York—Fiction. |
BISAC: FICTION / Legal. | FICTION / Thrillers. |
GSAFD: Legal stories. | Romans á clef.
Classification: LCC PS3612.I33526 B54 2017 | DDC 813/.6—dc23
LC record available at https://lccn.loc.gov/2016026671
p.   cm.

Printed in the United States of America
1   3   5   7   9   10   8   6   4   2

BOOK DESIGN BY AMANDA DEWEY

For Simma, still and always

"BigLaw" is an industry nickname for the nation's largest law firms. BigLaw firms are full-service law firms that traditionally:

- Employ large numbers of attorneys (100+);
- Rank among the top-grossing law firms in the nation;
- Pay top-market salaries;
- Recruit from tier one law schools;
- Maintain a national or global presence, with multiple offices across the country or the world.

—About.com Legal Careers Glossary

Size matters.

—Anonymous

PROLOGUE

I'm not much of a drinker.

"Another over here, please," I call to the barmaid.

She's good-looking, decked out in tight jeans with a shrink-wrap black top and, of course, tattoos. Tattoos and piercings. So common these days they hardly provoke a second glance.

My brother seated beside me raises and wiggles his empty glass.

"Me, too," he calls to her. "You lovely example of flowering womanhood," he adds, smiling that in-the-bag grin he gets when sloshed.

My brother, Sean, is drinking Jameson's. So far I'm sticking with beer. It's coming on to 11:00 a.m. I need to stay sober. (Okay, I'm not, but I'm not hammered either. Not yet anyway.) There's a jury out. We're waiting to see if the nine women and three men will reach a verdict today.

Yesterday the jury told the judge at the end of their second day of deliberations that they were deadlocked. He read them something lawyers call the Allen charge. It dates all the way back to 1896. *Allen v. United States*. Sometimes referred to as the dynamite charge.

The jury tells the judge they are hopelessly deadlocked and can't reach a verdict.

The judge tells the jury go back into the jury room and work on it some more, tells them—in so many words—get back in there, talk some more, and agree on a verdict. Do your fucking jobs.

Then, if the jury still can't agree, more often than not a mistrial is declared. The jury is excused and the defendant or defendants walk. Of course, the prosecutors can retry the case. Sometimes they do and sometimes they don't.

I sound like a lawyer?

"Thanks," I say to the barmaid as she places a new frosty mug in front of me. When she puts Sean's new whiskey down, he tells her how luscious she looks this morning. She raises her eyebrows, smiles, but no way is she falling for any of his bullshit.

Well, I am a lawyer. My brother isn't. He's a professional fuckup.

I've got to make this my last beer.

Sean and me are at Cahill's, one of the last Irish bars in this part of lower Manhattan where both the state and federal courthouses are located. I'd say the neighborhood is almost all Chinatown now.

We are the sons of Irish immigrants. Working-class people. Sean is upholding the tradition. In spades. Me? Well, I guess the priests saw something in me. They got me educated. Prep school rather than public or even Sacred Heart down our street. Full scholarship. Then college and law school. Also a free ride.

So you're thinking, here I am a lawyer waiting on a verdict and sitting here drinking with my brother while my client's fate is hanging in the balance, that the poor son of a bitch is off somewhere biting his nails while his world crumbles before his very eyes. That I must be one of those low-life criminal lawyers who hang around the halls of the local courthouse. Some schlub whose client roster is a collection of dopers, murderers, molesters, and whatnot.

Actually, that's not who or what I am. I was a young partner in the New York office of one of the most prominent law firms in the country.

I worked long and hard to get there. I've overcome my fair share of adversity.

And there is no client sitting somewhere biting his nails waiting for the jury.

I'm the client. I was the one indicted. It's *my* fate on the line.

My cell beeps. I remove it from my pocket. It's a text from my lawyer.

"The jury's in," I tell Sean. "They have a verdict."

He signals for the check.

TWO YEARS
EARLIER

1.

I didn't start taking notes right away.

It took me a while to figure out what was actually going on. Then I made sure to take notes.

I did it every morning, soon as I got out of bed. At first it was . . . I don't know, a self-preservation technique. I was afraid that I just wouldn't remember. So much was happening so fast.

I also figured that someday somebody—maybe another lawyer taking my deposition, questioning me under oath, or maybe bar ethics counsel—would expect me to recall all the important details. If the thought of a prosecutor entered my mind, I'm pretty sure I wiped it away before the ink was dry.

Writing this memoir? It actually wasn't my idea. It was my brother's. By that time most of the facts were out in the open. There were lawsuits, an SEC investigation, depositions, and document productions by the boatload. So I was able to piece together the story, pretty much all of it, from the events that I personally observed and a lot of what happened out of my presence.

I was just beginning my second year as a newly minted partner at Dunn & Sullivan. I had spent eight years working day and night as an associate attorney at the firm. Trust me when I tell you I was far from a shoo-in to make partner, let alone to last the full eight years as an associate.

Dunn & Sullivan's main office was in Manhattan. It also had offices in just about every major city in this country and throughout the world. At the time of this story, there were over twenty-five hundred lawyers on the payroll and another three thousand staff employees of one kind or another.

So my involvement with the story began on the day I was summoned to Carl Smith's office. Carl was the firm's chairman.

At the time I had only a nodding relationship with Chairman Smith. He'd nod to me in the elevator, in the firm's cafeteria, in the halls. Never said a word. Did he even know my name? Turns out he did.

I got to his office at the appointed hour. His door was shut. His secretary was away from her desk. I stood there deciding, should I knock or should I wait for the secretary to return?

I decided to knock, and just as I raised my fist, the door flew open and a bull of a senior partner named Richard Miller stormed past me with enough force that we knocked shoulders.

When I was still an associate, I had worked on several of Miller's cases. What a miserable prick. He brutalized everyone who worked under him. Around the office he was known as "Mad Dog" Miller.

I watched him bombard his way down the hall. He seemed to be clutching a single sheet of paper. He was a big guy, barrel-chested, with steel-rimmed glasses and a Teddy Roosevelt mustache. Like I said, a bull of a man. I've seen Miller in the locker room of our firm's fitness center. (Yes, we have our own fitness center in the building.) Naked, he's got a pair of chicken legs holding up that massive upper frame.

"Mr. Blake? Carney?"

I turned at that. Carl Smith calling my name. I poked my head in his open doorway.

"Sir?" I said, feeling stupid. We were law partners. Shouldn't I be calling him Carl?

"Come in. Have a seat."

So I did.

Mr. Smith . . . Carl . . . was seated behind this massive, ornate partner's desk. Something Napoleon could have owned.

Dunn & Sullivan's New York office, the command center for the entire firm, was located in this spanking new glass-and-steel tower stuck right smack in the middle of Times Square. This was the new Times Square. Gone were the strip joints and porn emporiums. It had become a choice business address.

Carl Smith's office looked like the nineteenth century embedded in the twenty-first. There must have been a small fortune of antique furniture in there.

I sat on one of the two needlepoint chairs across from him. At first, Smith said nothing. He seemed to be studying me. Considering.

"You're a third-year, right?"

"Second." (I think I mumbled "Sir.")

Smith shrugged. He looked at me some more. Did he need a third-year partner for whatever he had in mind? Was I about to be dismissed?

I leaned forward, sort of ready to spring to my feet and leave, when Smith reached over to the corner of his desk and picked up an iPad.

I watched as he did some forefinger tapping on the screen. Then I heard the whoosh.

"Sent you a file."

Okay? And?

He kept looking at me. I kept looking at him. What was on his mind? And why was I so fucking nervous?

Carl Smith was a legend in his own time. He came from humble beginnings. Like me.

His father was a German immigrant, a laborer, so the story went.

His mother came from a large Staten Island working-class Italian family. She was the one with the smarts. Carl back then was still Karl Schmidt Jr. After his father, Karl Sr.

Carl cut a wide path around his stern father but adored his mother, who raised him in the Catholic faith. Until he entered Yale (on scholarship), Carl was very *Italian*, a mama's boy with a German name. The Ivy League changed all that. He became a synthetic patrician. The full monty. That was when he legally changed his name.

After law school (Harvard), followed by his clerkship for a United States Supreme Court justice, he joined Dunn & Sullivan as an associate. Made partner after five years. No one had done that before, or has since.

Welcome to the world of Big Law. A world run by men like Carl Smith. (Mostly) white men with brilliant minds and easy smiles that at once conceal and reveal their true nature: they're predators.

Big Law is selective. Hard to get in. Even harder to stay in.

The country's leading law firms recruit new lawyers each and every year. Almost exclusively from the best law schools. Mostly from the big three: Harvard, Yale, Stanford. Top-of-the-class students graduating from state law schools and so-called second-tier law schools do also get hired, though in smaller numbers.

I was first in my class at Rutgers University's law school. I made the cut.

From the first day I stepped into the offices of Dunn & Sullivan, I got the distinct impression that I was cannon fodder. That I was there to work my ass off, but there was no way someone like me would be allowed to go the distance. The obligatory (except for Carl) eight years before eligibility for partnership selection.

I was an outsider. In the club, but only as a guest.

Work my ass off I did. On every assignment. Did my job no matter what, no matter how long it took, or how many times I had to do it over.

I beat the odds. Made partner on my first try. But know what? That feeling of otherness, of not being one of them?

Still there.

I'm a big guy. Not overweight. Just big. I love my Irish roots. I've got dark, curly hair and dark eyes. I grew up lower-class, what back then was called "shanty Irish" or, given my looks, "black Irish." Now I suppose I'd be called "lace-curtain Irish."

I could dress a little better, could keep my ties more tightly tucked under my shirt collar. And I still speak in a working-class New Yorkese. I could change that. Drop the accent. But I don't. In some way I can't really articulate, it defines me.

Carl Smith (still checking me out) was my opposite. He was small-boned and oh, so very neat. Brioni suits (I later learned), crisp designer ties, perfectly coiffed hair. And not even a trace of Staten Island in his speech. Then Carl said:

"Here's what I want you to do. Read that file. It's a plaintiffs' class-action case. You have handled class actions before, right?"

And I had.

Class-action cases contain a large number of claimants who have the facts and law in common. The courts allow all the plaintiffs to join together in one lawsuit rather than having umpteen lawsuits litigating the same case over and over and over.

I had been a member of several class-action trial teams. But Dunn & Sullivan had always been on the defendants' side of these cases. Never the plaintiffs'. Typically the defendants were the corporate bad guys: The drillers. The spillers. The killers.

Yes, those were our clients. The best lawyers for the worst offenders. That's the system. Everyone is entitled to legal representation. Bad guys included. Otherwise there is no system.

Okay, so Smith wants to take on the plaintiffs' side. The good guys for a change. Fine with me.

So I nodded, *yeah, I have*. (It would be nice if that cat would come back with my tongue.)

"Okay. Learn the file, then put together your trial team."

My trial team?

As though Smith read my thoughts:

"I am placing you in charge of this case. Everyone on it will report to you. You will report to me. But you will be in charge of all day-to-day activities."

Up until then I hadn't been in charge of anything. Junior partners were not placed in charge of major cases. Yet Smith was placing me in charge of one.

Something wasn't adding up.

I quickly flushed that thought down the drain. Instead my thinking went along these lines:

Carl Smith had seen something in me that caused him to ignore firm practice and put me in charge of a major case (the firm chairman didn't personally assign minor cases). This despite my relative lack of experience.

Maybe it was our similar childhoods? Maybe he had a soft spot in his heart for up-from-the-street achievers like he was?

Then again, Carl Smith didn't have a heart.

He did have this false charm. Something he could play like the proverbial Stradivarius when he chose to, though he never did for me.

So I was sitting there feeling pretty good about myself. Totally missing Smith's body language signaling that the meeting was over. That it was time for me to leave.

"Thank you," he finally said.

No, thank you, I was about to say when I realized I was being dismissed. ("Thank you" was spelled "good-bye.")

This time it was me who nodded at Carl Smith. Then I got up and left.

2.

So I was back in my broom closet of an office.

I spent the rest of the day reading Smith's e-mailed file. It was a doozy of a case. It looked like the case had come in through a young Indian lawyer who had handled it in his home country but now needed help from an American law firm.

Of course, that wasn't the real story.

The case was a monkey trap. (I'll explain in a minute.) It began with another lawyer named Peter Moss.

And who was he?

A Harvard Law School classmate of Carl's. They didn't get along. Not then, not ever.

Peter Moss had accepted a post-law-school offer from Dunn & Sullivan. Two years later, after Carl Smith's Supreme Court clerkship ended, he also came to Dunn & Sullivan. From the start they were oil and water. Two young associate attorneys in heavy competition for a hard-to-get partnership.

The partners at the time were amused by their rivalry. These two bright and aggressive young lawyers neck and neck, racing to the finish line, jostling each other at every available opportunity.

And then Peter was brought into a supervising partner's office and told he had no future at the firm. Just like that he was out of a job. And to make matters worse, an innuendo of bothersome behavior clung to his abrupt departure like chewing gum to the sole of a shoe.

Peter was convinced that Smith's invisible hand had pushed him out the door. Carl was an absolute master of behind-the-scenes maneuvering, a regular Svengali. The partners had done the firing, but Peter was convinced that Carl was the snitch.

There was nothing specific, only a murky rumor. But it was enough. Peter had difficulty finding another job.

Was it true? The bad behavior?

Probably not.

The best that Peter Moss could do was a modest, midsize law firm in Washington, D.C. He sucked it up, accepted the offer (at considerably less pay), and moved his young family to the District.

And he gave it his all. In addition to being very smart, Peter was a good-looking, engaging guy. Just over six feet tall, he kept his wiry build with YMCA indoor-pool laps, much as he had done on his high-school and college swim teams. His stick-straight sandy hair and bright eyes gave him a familiarity that clients found reassuring.

So he threw himself into his new firm. It didn't take long before he had risen to a position of leadership. And then he set about growing the firm. Taking a page out of the playbook of Wall Street's mergers-and-acquisitions gurus, Peter acquired other law firms, and before long he sat at the head of a Big Law contender.

As the firm ballooned in size, Peter opened an office in New York, then Chicago, then Miami, and so on. And then he set his sights on Dunn & Sullivan.

After all, Peter had a score to settle.

And so the monkey trap.

3.

You need a sealed box with a coconut in it.

You cut a hole in the box large enough for the monkey's hand but too small to prevent the coconut from being removed from inside the box. The monkey has his arm through the hole, his fist around the delicious coconut, but he can't get the coconut out. The monkey holds on to the coconut. The monkey gets caught.

If the new case was the coconut, Peter Moss figured Carl Smith for the monkey.

There was a method to Peter's madness. This was more than vindictiveness. Sure, he wanted to settle a score, but Peter had indeed become a "Wall Street" type. It was inevitable. Commercial law was all about big business. Gone were the days of practicing law like some kind of country doctor.

Mason Rose (that was the name of Peter's law firm) needed to grow. A takeover of Dunn & Sullivan would catapult them squarely into the majors. To survive you needed big clients with big cases who paid big bucks for their legal representation. Peter had kept his eye on

Carl Smith's law firm. He considered it an underperformer stock. So he was first going to hobble it. Then gobble it.

But could he pull it off? He thought so. He also knew his enemy. While his firm might be in trouble, Carl Smith was a formidable opponent. There were definite risks here. As the saying goes, if you take a shot at the king, you'd better kill him. Otherwise he'll kill you.

So what was this case about?

GRE, for General Renewable Energy, was part of an American conglomerate whose sticky corporate fingers were in many pots. This one was natural gas.

When GRE's gas plant in the Assam region of India blew, the American and European managers delayed employee evacuation, hoping to put a lid on what was already an uncontrollable situation.

Some of the recovered bodies were burned to a crisp. For those who survived, toxic-chemical inhalation affected lungs and central nervous systems. A cloud of poisoned air descended on the nearby villages where the workers' families lived. It was a horrible mess.

The company quickly settled claims for environmental damage brought by the Indian government. Its compensation offers to its impoverished Indian workforce and their families were far less generous. There was also some evidence of sabotage. The company brass thought a cabal of workers were the culprits. There was no way they were going to reward them for this with big payouts.

A young Indian lawyer named Dipak Singh, trying to make an independent name for himself as the youngest member of a Brahman family of lawyers and jurists, took on the case for the workers and their families. (And so the "class" of the class-action suit was established. This was the Indian legal version, a cousin to the American legal version.)

Indian justice was swift. It was also slippery.

Jury trials had been abolished in India, so a single judge in the local court of Guwahati, the closest city to the plant, heard the case.

The company lost big-time. At the current exchange rate of Indian rupees to U.S. dollars, the judgment was just shy of two and a half billion dollars. That's right: *billion*.

GRE refused to pay up and had begun an investigation into just how the case ended as it had. (Possible improprieties hadn't yet come to light. But there were rumors. Among them the strong ties between the judge and the powerful Singh family.) It shuttered its plant and self-sabotaged its equipment. So company assets in the U.S. and elsewhere had to be seized by the judgment plaintiffs and then sold off to satisfy the Indian court's monetary award.

Dipak Singh needed to file suit in the U.S. to seize GRE's corporate assets. For that he needed a U.S. law firm. Dunn & Sullivan got the job. The case looked good to Carl Smith. It could last for years, and the fees earned would be humongous. GRE had retained Peter Moss and Mason Rose to defend them against these seizures.

But there was some real skulduggery going on. As I later learned, Peter had paid Dipak under the table for him to retain Dunn & Sullivan as the plaintiffs' American counsel. That's right. Peter Moss had secretly selected his own adversary. Why? Part of the plan. Peter's scheme to topple Dunn & Sullivan.

So Dipak came to New York and met with Smith. He sat in the very same needlepoint chair that I occupied the next day when Smith tapped me to head the case.

When they were later interrogated about that meeting, they told different stories.

What a shocker. But when you put the two stories together, examine them side by side, you can figure out what really happened.

4.

"offee?"

"Tea, actually."

Smith buzzed his secretary. Dipak Singh's tea came quickly enough for Smith to endure small talk (*Good flight? Been to New York before?*) only briefly.

What was Carl expecting in this Indian lawyer? Who knows? Our law firm's chairman was unquestionably urbane and polished, a cultivated and highly educated man. Yet when it came to preconceived notions about people, the upper crust harbored the same kind of ethnic and racial bias you'd expect to see in some low-life dunce. Carl Smith masked it well, but cultural tolerance was not among his finer points.

So what was he expecting? Some subservient and ingratiating dark-skinned Indian in a cheap suit spouting singsongy, accented colonial English? If he was, that's not what he got.

Sitting across from him was a young man with an unmistakably regal bearing. And while there were definite traces of a subcontinental accent in his speech, his enunciation was straight out of Oxford University, where he had completed his law studies. He was young, about the same age as a first-year Dunn & Sullivan associate, with powdery beige Brahman skin, gray eyes, ruler-straight, side-parted thick black hair. He was Savile Row–suited, sporting a fashionable five-o'clock-shadowed stubble shave and a beautiful though oversize gold watch on his hairy left wrist. This kid lawyer looked like he'd be perfectly at ease sipping tea in the presence of the queen of England.

And while Carl was studying Dipak, Dipak was studying Carl. This American senior partner dressed to the nines behind his massive desk in this mausoleum of an office.

Dipak had something Carl wanted. So Carl switched on his patented charm.

"I've read your e-mail and the case-file attachments you sent along with it," he said, beaming, as Dipak replaced his teacup on the edge of Carl's desk.

Carl reached into a side drawer, retrieved a coaster, and slid it under Dipak's saucer. Dipak's smile of thanks seemed more in tune for a servant's actions than for a law firm chairman's. This was not lost on Carl.

"It is, I assure you, a very good case," Dipak said.

"Of that I have no doubt," Carl assured him, adding, "We are pleased that you have chosen us for this assignment."

The fact was that Carl Smith desperately needed to bring in some substantial legal fees. The recent recession had upended things. Corporate clients had begun questioning their legal expenses, many requiring reductions and discounts if their law firms wanted to keep their business. Client loyalty had disappeared. Legal work went to the lowest bidder. Carl's law firm was hurting, though none of this was public yet.

Carl Smith guarded Dunn & Sullivan's books like a sentry in a combat zone.

"You are wondering perhaps how I acquired this case?" Dipak asked.

Not only didn't Carl wonder, he didn't give a shit.

But he should have.

As we all later learned, Dipak took the case on what we American lawyers call a contingent fee. Meaning that Dipak was paid nothing by these dirt-poor peasant workers and their families. He would take his fee as a percentage of any and all money recovered. The problem was that in India contingent-fee arrangements between lawyers and their clients were strictly forbidden.

Our enterprising Dipak Singh had circumvented this prohibition by on paper fictitiously "lending" his clients the money with which to hire him. He also had a secret side agreement for a percentage share of the award. Fifty percent of every rupee/dollar recovered. Totally unacceptable in the U.S., where a third of any recovery was the norm, and for cases of this magnitude the percentage would be even smaller. Carl would have been shocked had he known that Dipak stood to receive fifty cents on every dollar collected.

Can you imagine? Dipak becomes a billionaire off one case? And he, too, needed the money. Dipak's family might have enjoyed Indian high-caste status, but when it came to actual earnings, a string of careless investments had drained the coffers of his father and each and every one of his uncles. The kid was broke and overly ambitious. Sometimes a good combination. Sometimes not.

While contingent-fee arrangements were commonplace in the U.S., the major law firms did not normally take on such work. Their clients paid by the hour, and that was what funded the firms' day-to-day operations. Carl knew there was no money here until GRE's assets were seized by court order and then liquidated. But he knew how to handle the pay-as-you-go problem.

Hedge funds, always in search of new markets to score outlandish profits, had focused on litigation financing. Lending money to law firms to finance cases where up-front money simply wasn't available and at interest rates that were sky-high and therefore unlawful if the loan had come from a bank.

But hedge funds weren't banks. Regulatory Washington was once again asleep at the wheel. Litigation finance was the new next-best thing for law firms.

So Big Law took a high-board dive into the deep waters of OPM (other people's money) to bet on legal case outcomes. And the hedge funds showered money on the law firms in what was called "non-recourse" financing. Meaning if the case was lost, the law firm owed nothing further on the money it borrowed. The loan was wiped off its books, and the hedge fund took the hit.

How could they do this and survive? Sky-high interest-rate payments were demanded and regularly remitted by the law firms as the cases wound their often years-long slog through the courts.

There was more.

On increasing occasions big law firms took to adding a kicker to their hourly rates. It was in the form of what was called a "success fee." A bonus earned for a favorable result. The hedge funds would take a portion of that success fee. So between monthly interest payments and their share of success fees, incoming money was large enough to offset any funds lost on unsuccessful cases.

Big Law had placed its invisible hand on the blackboard eraser and began smoothing away the chalk line between lawyering as a profession and lawyering as Wall Street wheeling and dealing.

While Carl was thinking about this, Dipak Singh was explaining how resourceful he had been to take on this case but providing next to no detail. Carl was tuned out. Then Dipak came back into range.

"There are many GRE assets in your country and also in Europe that can be seized."

"And we will have them seized as quickly as possible."

"As to your fee. May I call you Carl . . . ?"

A delighted *by all means* nod. An *if you must* thought.

There was something about this cheerful senior partner entertaining him, something Dipak couldn't quite put his finger on, that didn't square with the bubbly enthusiasm. He decided to forgo any informality.

"I would propose for your firm a substantial success fee of ten percent of all monies recovered above your hourly rates."

The math here was easy. Ten percent of two and a half billion was two hundred and fifty million. More than enough on its own to pay whatever interest was charged on the litigation-finance loan needed to satisfy hourly rate charges and put a very healthy sum on the law firm's books. Win-win.

Carl wanted this case in the firm's accounts as soon as possible. It would be the largest single legal fee that Dunn & Sullivan had ever received. There was already a judgment. The Indian court had spoken. This was a mop-up operation. Find company assets, then use the courts to seize and sell them? Candy from a baby.

And it fit in nicely with Carl's exit strategy.

Yes, he had an exit strategy.

But I'm getting ahead of myself.

Carl was going to take on this case. Anyone looking at Dunn & Sullivan's balance sheet would see this money-in-the-bank asset. Not yet realized, but just around the corner.

In his zeal to haul the GRE case on board, Carl didn't stop to consider the odds of this young Indian lawyer, dashing though he might have been, hitting the home run of home runs with what was likely his first real case. Instead he mentally searched Dunn & Sullivan's young-lawyer roster, looking for the right kind of junior partner to run the case: someone relatively inexperienced, eager to head up an asset-seizure litigation team. Someone who wouldn't ask too many questions.

That would be me.

Peter Moss and his law firm? At that point light-years away from Carl's radar screen.

So Carl Smith closed his fist around the coconut.

5.

I should be married.

What I mean is that I would like to be married. Have a family.

I'm thirty-seven years old. I can easily afford a family. But that's not the point. What I'm trying to say is that my life is one-dimensional.

My brother keeps asking me, *Where's the Porsche?*

It's an inside joke. He's flat broke. And here I am. Loaded and spending none of it.

I don't even own a car. Who needs a car in New York City?

My life as a young partner is marginally better than when I was an associate, but I'm still at the office, or on a plane to some other office or courthouse, all the time. I have a nice enough apartment in one of the new high-rise rentals on the far West Side of the city, at Sixty-second Street and West End Avenue. I'm on the top floor and have a fairly decent Hudson River view. I still haven't hung anything on my walls.

I'm not asking you to play an imaginary fiddle over my "poor and unfortunate" situation. I've come a long way, and I am proud of myself for what I've accomplished.

My brother and I grew up in a section of Manhattan called Hell's Kitchen. It's also on the far West Side, between Thirty-fourth and Fifty-ninth Streets bounded by Eighth Avenue and the Hudson.

To this day six-story walk-ups still line the streets, but they now contain remodeled apartments with state-of-the-art kitchens, central air, and recessed lighting.

Back when my brother and I were kids, the neighborhood was different. The Westies gang—friends of the infamous Colombo mob—still ruled the streets. Irish immigrants and their families lived in the walk-ups. Hell's Kitchen was not a nice place.

Our apartment was rent-controlled. Still is. My brother lives there with our dad. One of the few like that left in the neighborhood. I pay the rent, but my brother pays the price. Our dad, Seamus, is a handful.

Belfast born and bred, he had for years been a doorman at a Park Avenue co-op and was far nicer to the children of its wealthy residents than he ever was to his own boys. He was all smiles and gentle comments during the day, while surly drunk and quick with the back of his hand at night.

Our mother tolerated him, staying that hand against his boys only when he lost all control. While she was alive, our dad took her for granted. Her cancer went undiagnosed long enough to bring on a quick death. My dad no longer works. Now he spends both days *and* nights in a bottle.

Sean, my brother, is the chain that keeps me tethered. He never lets me forget who I am. He's older by three years. He always looked out for me. Let me fight my own fights as a kid, but I knew he was there for me if I needed him. And now that Sean is broken, I will—no matter what—be there for him.

Honorably discharged from the marines after three combat tours, his right leg saved by battlefield triage, disfigured but workable, otherwise not a mark on him. At least on the outside.

Had Sean's helmet strap not held, flying shrapnel from the exploding IED would have shorn off the top of his head. But its concussive effect had him lying in the road near the smoldering wreckage of his personnel carrier, immobile, helpless.

He watched the insurgents appear from out of nowhere. Saw them stand over the other two marines who just moments ago had been in the personnel carrier with him. They, too, were still alive, but down like him.

One of the insurgents was holding a gasoline can. Sean watched him pour from it, soaking the other two marines' fatigues, and then flick on his lighter and toss it at them. He heard their screams of agony. Sean says the smell of their burning flesh is still with him.

He continued watching as one of the insurgents noticed him. Had he been shouting at them? The guy, turbaned, but in jeans and a Gap T-shirt, calmly walked over to Sean, studied him, and then raised his weapon, aiming it point-blank at his face. The guy said something in Arabic as Sean clenched his eyes shut, waiting for oblivion.

The track of automatic-weapons fire from the rescuing helicopter tore into the insurgent before he could finish the job. The others then quickly fled.

Horrible as it was, that wasn't the worst of it.

Days before that patrol, Sean's commanding officer had ordered him to fire at a young girl coming toward them in the Kandahar province village they were sweeping. The officer was certain she had a suicide vest strapped inside her clothes. He'd shouted at her in English to halt, not one step further. And when the young girl kept walking, he shouted his order to Sean.

Sean fired a quick burst into her, watched as the shells lacerated her body, instantly turning her into a bloody mess.

As she lay there on the ground twitching, Sean approached and used his rifle muzzle to poke at her middle. Nothing. The girl had on nothing but the powder-blue burka typical of women in this region of Afghanistan. She looked about twelve, no older.

Sean's officer walked away as though nothing had happened. My brother knelt by the girl until she stopped breathing. At one point, just before the officer was out of range, he raised his weapon and sighted it on him but lowered it without firing.

Sean came home and then was set adrift. He goes to the VA from time to time to meet with a military shrink. Can't see that it's doing him any good. He's had a series of jobs. All menial. Hasn't been able to hold any of them.

My brother's girlfriend, Rosy, grew up on our block. Same Irish roots. She and Sean fell in love probably in the sixth grade. Rosy was a drunk, and worse, but she truly loved my brother. She lived in the apartment with him and Seamus.

I do date occasionally. Like lots of single people my age who have precious little opportunity to meet someone outside work, I've met and dated women through online matchmaker sites. Until the last woman I met, I would have said it was a waste of time.

She was the exception that proved the rule. Really smart. Good-looking. And black.

No, not black Irish. Black black.

Our third time out, I arranged a dinner for us with Sean and Rosy. I chose an upscale restaurant, a place my brother and Rosy would never go to on their own.

That could have been a mistake.

6.

I'm a meat-and-potatoes guy. Sean is, too.

So I reserved a table for four at Keens Steakhouse, one of the city's oldest restaurants. Since it's on Thirty-sixth Street between Fifth and Sixth Avenues, I could easily walk there from work. (I planned to return to the office after dinner.)

Keens is dark-paneled, 1890s-looking. Definitely not a part of hip New York. But the steaks are big and juicy, the wine list long (and pricey).

So we all agreed to meet in the restaurant's bar at 7:15 p.m. for a 7:30 reservation. I got there first. Sean hadn't met my date yet, and I wanted to be there for the introductions. The bar was already packed. Lined up two and three deep were a bunch of mostly young white guys in suits. By the looks of them, lawyers, stockbrokers, hedge-funders all. The drinking was serious. The bar loud and tight.

I saw Sean and Rosy at the entrance, Sean on tiptoes searching for me. It was early November and cold in New York. I'd worn a topcoat that I had checked. Sean was dressed like Sean. No coat or jacket, a hoodie, loose jeans, and sneakers. I could see that Rosy had made some effort to dress up. She had on jeans, too, but with a nicer top than she usually wore; her navy-surplus pea coat was carefully folded over her arm.

I signaled them from where I was standing at the far end of the bar. The guys standing next to me turned their heads. I noticed but paid it no mind. I watched as Sean guided Rosy through the crowd. When they got to me, Rosy first, she held out her arms for the double-cheeked kiss I always got from her. Sean must have knocked into one of those guys standing next to me. I heard him apologize. I saw the guy look Sean up and down, then turn his back on him. I couldn't see if Sean had noticed that.

"Hey," Sean said as we bear-hugged.

In appearance my brother and I were two sides of the same coin. Clearly related, with the same dark eyes and curly hair, the same-shaped face. I was far from manicured in appearance, but I did look the part for what I had become. Unfortunately, so did Sean. Rough hands, chewed fingernails, too many tattoos. His beaming Irish smile showing a missing tooth.

I watched Rosy look around, obviously pleased to be here. She was already drunk. Or stoned. I could see it. Her eyes were glassy, and she wasn't all that steady.

Rosy had once been attractive. Pretty face, good figure, but the wear and tear of her life had left its mark. Now she was dumpy, anemic-looking, also heavily tattooed. Her hair was cut boyishly short, dyed a severe black, while premature gray roots peeked out from her center part. But Rosy was still as pleasant and sweet as could be.

I got the bartender's attention and motioned for two more of what I was having. (I was drinking Heineken draft.) He quickly drew them and placed the pint glasses on the bar in front of me. I gave one each to Sean and Rosy.

"Cheers," Sean said, raising his glass in salute.

Just then the guy Sean had bumped into took a step backward, guffawing at something one of his compadres had said, and went right into Sean's glass, spilling beer down the front of his sweatshirt. The guy had to have noticed what he'd done, but he kept his back to Sean. Sean looked at himself, brushed excess beer from the front of his hoodie, and left it at that.

I was about to say something to this guy, but Sean signaled no to me.

"Hi."

And there was my date, standing in front of us.

After introductions we made our way into the restaurant proper and our table.

So we're eating, first-course salads and a shared plate of raw oysters gone. Main-course steaks for three of us. A vegetable plate for my date.

Note to self: Ask your dates if they eat meat before making restaurant reservations.

She didn't seem to mind. And I was pleased (and relieved) that Sean and Rosy took to her so quickly. Her being black? As far as I could tell, they couldn't have cared less. Remember, we were all from Hell's Kitchen. Not a part of the city known for its tolerance back then. No way would I introduce this very nice person sitting next to me, laughing at Sean's banter, to my father. That would be a disaster.

Okay, so who is this person?

Her name is Diane Robichaud. She was born and raised in Lake Charles, Louisiana. Came to New York for college (Hunter) and stayed for law school (NYU). Must be something in my online profile that attracts women lawyers—this is my third so far.

She's tall, an inch or two over me, kind of lanky, and beautiful. Nut-brown skin and green eyes. A legacy, was the way she put it, from the plantation slave master's taking a fancy to one of her ancestors. And she's funny.

Her dad was career army, so Sean liked that. Diane worked in lower Manhattan as an assistant district attorney in the local criminal court, though she lives in Queens. Her city-government salary was not nearly enough for a decent apartment in Manhattan, or for that matter in the newly chic sections of Brooklyn that so many young (and well-paid) professionals have colonized.

We were having a nice time. I had ordered a good Napa cabernet. (Sean and Rosy stayed with beer.) The waiter was topping up Diane's glass. The same guys who'd stood next to us at the bar had taken the table directly across from us, against the wall. When they were being seated, I noticed one nudge the other, lifting his chin: *Take a look at them.*

Meaning, of course, us.

And I guess we did stand out a little. Two badly dressed white people. Clearly lower class. The nicely dressed black girl with the suited white guy. But they took their seats and settled in. Or so I thought.

We were at a round table. Rosy had her back to where these guys were seated, as I said, against the wall. They were at a rectangular table. Sean was facing them; Diane and I had side views. The time or two I casually glanced over, I could see that they were still at the hard stuff, their waiter bringing over more rounds of cocktails even though they, too, were at their steaks.

Rosy was eating, though really pecking at her food, downing beers instead. She hadn't said much but was enjoying herself, and I especially liked the way she was with Diane, evidently impressed by this woman lawyer.

And then.

One of the guys from the other table got up and came over to us. Bending just slightly, some faux posture of friendliness, he said, "Excuse me, folks." Touching Rosy lightly on the shoulder.

"My friends over there," he said, smiling, very drunk. "Well, one of them thinks he may have gone to boarding school with you. Phillips Exeter?"

Rosy turned in her seat and looked over at that table. One of those with his back to the wall, stupid grin, wiggling his fingers: *Hi there.*

Rosy got it. But she simply turned back in her seat to face us. She was staring at the table. Ridiculed.

"No?" The guy said to Rosy. Pushing it. "You sure?"

There was sniggering at the other table.

"Okay," the guy said. "Our mistake. Enjoy your dinner." And returned to his own table. Retook his seat. His back to us.

More laughter, then I saw Mr. Finger Wiggler take out his wallet and pass some bills to the guy who had come to our table.

And that's when Sean got up.

Rosy didn't turn around, but Diane and I could see.

He walked over to their table. Leaned into the face of the guy who'd been at our table. I saw Sean put his hand in his jeans pocket and then start speaking in a voice too low for us to hear from where we were seated. The guy's back was to us, so I couldn't see his face, but I clearly saw him stiffen. The others at the table were no longer amused. Grim faces all around.

When he finished, Sean straightened up. We watched the guy get up and then walk right out of the dining room. Not so much as a glance our way. Sean came back to our table. One of the others still at their table signaled the waiter for the check. Keep in mind they, too, were in mid-meal.

The check arrived, it was quickly settled, and then the rest of them got up and left the restaurant. Filing right by us, eyes elsewhere.

Sean winked at Rosy. Letting her know. All okay now.

"What did you say to them?" Diane asked.

"Oh," Sean said, shrugging. "They had somewhere else they had to be. I was just reminding them of that."

"Where else?" Diane asked.

"Anywhere else," Sean said as he sliced off a big chunk of steak and ate it. "Great place, bro," chewing, he said to me. "Let's come back here sometime."

Diane and I exchanged glances. She raised her eyebrows. Nodded. Yeah, let's. Okay, so maybe it wasn't a mistake coming here.

And what was it that my brother said to that guy?

By then we'd finished dinner and were back out on Sixth Avenue headed for the subway for them and the office for me. Diane and Rosy were a few paces ahead of us, delightedly gabbing.

"What'd you say to him?" I asked Sean when I could see we were out of earshot.

He hunched his shoulders, like it was no big deal.

"Nothing much," he said. "Just told the motherfucker now that he'd insulted my girl, I felt honor-bound to hurt him. You know, like with the knife in my pocket, telling him maybe . . . I don't know, I'd stab him in the balls or slice off a piece of his ear. One or the other. Needed to fuck him up 'cause of what he did. Told him that."

"What'd he say?"

"Nothing. Oh, yeah, I also told him if he left that very second, got his sorry ass out of there, I'd let him be. Told him his buddies needed to leave, too. But I said they needed to decide real fast, 'cause I was kind of hot right at the moment."

"Come on," I said. "You weren't going to do anything. In the middle of a fucking restaurant?"

Sean looked at me. Even under the streetlights, I could see something in his eyes, something very dark that wasn't there when we were kids. Something post-military.

"Nah," Sean said after a while, winking at me. "I was just saying."

I didn't believe him.

And that frightened me.

7.

I spent the next several weeks working on the new case.

The weather got even colder. New York slides from fall to winter like a runner into a stolen base. Not there. Then there. Coats get heavier, and the knit hats and scarves come out.

My apartment was close enough to Times Square for me to walk to work. I liked that. It gave me time to think. Even in the cold.

My plan was to file the first lawsuit in New York. Get a judgment authorizing asset seizures and then use that case as precedent for other cases we'd file elsewhere in the U.S. and abroad.

I called Carl Smith. Got his secretary. Told her I would like an appointment to sit down with the big man and brief him. She said she'd pass on the message. Later that day she called back to tell me Mr. Smith had said no need for a meeting, I should just do what I needed to do.

And since our initial conference I hadn't seen him.

Correction.

I happened to be on his floor and needed to pee. Smith was coming out of the men's room just as I was going in. He inadvertently handed off the door to me. I stopped. Waited. Expecting something from him. *How's the case going? Making progress?*

Nothing. He nodded at me.

I stood there holding the door and watched him walk down the hall. There wasn't a crease in his tailor-made suit. Not a hair out of place. He was perfect.

I felt the pressure of being in charge of my new case. My office hours were getting even longer than usual.

I did make time for Diane. Her hours weren't great either. A prosecutor's life isn't a walk in the park. We'd have late-night dinners or earlier dinners with us both returning to our offices. I've stayed over at her place, and she's done the same at mine.

It was just before Thanksgiving. I was in Queens. At Diane's. Couldn't sleep and didn't want to wake her, so I went into the combination living room–dining area–kitchen of her tiny one-bedroom. The clock on the microwave told me it was 2:45 a.m.

Diane's apartment was in a place called Long Island City. It's not a city (though it once was), and it's in the borough of Queens though technically, I think, it may actually be a part of Long Island. LIC is located right on the East River with spectacular views of the Manhattan skyline, much like its richer cousin Williamsburg in Brooklyn. It once was a really rough place, run by a notorious Irish Boss Tweed sort of guy colorfully named Patrick "Battle-Axe" Gleason. Those days were long gone by the time Diane moved into one of the new high-rise buildings dotting the waterfront.

She had been an early tenant, taking an upper-floor water-view apartment before anyone wanted to live there. Since then LIC has become increasingly fashionable with the well-heeled, though non-filthy-rich, segment of New York's ever-present upwardly mobile classes. Rents were skyrocketing. Diane was already looking to move, unable on her modest government salary to withstand the next rent hike.

So I was on the thirty-first floor, standing at the window, facing the East River, directly across from Manhattan. I was staring out at her magnificent skyline view, wearing only boxers and a Rutgers T-shirt. Diane was off in the morning to Lake Charles and her family for Thanksgiving. I wasn't invited. I didn't expect her to ask me, but still . . .

Would I have gone if she had? Did she not invite me because we weren't there yet in our relationship? Or was there another reason? *The* other reason.

Thus far she and I had only tiptoed around race. An elephant in the room? I don't know. What I *did* know was that she was beautiful, sensitive, and charming. We seemed compatible. Getting to intimate didn't take long. And that had been good, too.

Was I kidding myself? I saw the looks of some people passing us on the street. No doubt far fewer than years ago. And not necessarily looks of disdain. Just noting the difference. Yeah, well, so what? Still, race was one of those "you can run, but you can't hide" kind of things.

It was on my mind that night. Was that why I couldn't sleep? Or was it the case? Whatever it was, it was now 3:00 a.m., and I was staring out the window.

So was Carl Smith.

In fact, in some screwy way we were staring at each other.

Really?

Well, not exactly, but get this.

8.

Carl Smith had sold his luxury prewar Upper East Side apartment for a fortune and then had put another small fortune into a newly opened steel-and-glass needle of an apartment building at 432 Park Avenue, a structure so high (eighty-five floors) that it looked down on the blocks-away Empire State Building.

Carl's new Manhattan apartment was on the thirty-first floor, level with Diane's in Long Island City. Even Carl couldn't afford to live on one of the above-the-clouds floors of his new building. Apartments up there went from $85 to $100 million. Who owned those? Russian oligarchs, Arab sheikhs, Chinese billionaires, with probably the occasional thirty-something American hedge-funder thrown in for good measure. City records showed that Carl paid $17.5 million for his place.

So it's 3:00 a.m. Carl's awake, like me. Staring out the window across the East River, right in my direction. His wife's asleep. More accurately, out cold.

Tonight, like most nights, Polly Smith had drunk herself into a stupor. How do I know this?

Their divorce-case record. And I can come pretty close to pinpointing the particular night in question. Polly remembered that night. Carl gave her reason to. Here's what she said in her deposition:

She awoke, alone in the bed. Her illuminated night-table alarm telling her it was 3:00 a.m. She turned on the light and pulled back the covers. She had wet her side of the bed. Again. She slid her way to the floor and walked out of the bedroom. She saw a thin sliver of light coming from under the door to the second bedroom. The one Carl had outfitted as his study. (There had been only one child to this frazzled marriage, and she had been estranged for years.)

Carl slept in pajamas, custom-made by Brioni, like his suits (the divorce case again). Polly squeezed the door open, and there stood Carl in his silks, deep in thought, looking out the window across the East River. She took a barefooted step or two into the room.

Polly, this doyenne of New York society, in her urine-soaked nightgown. Groggy. Still half drunk.

"Carl?"

He kept his back to her.

"Go back to bed."

She took a few steps closer to her husband.

"Carl?"

This was an important night. Carl had come to a final decision. His exit strategy from Dunn & Sullivan was about to be put into play. He had been standing there thinking this through very carefully.

"Carl?"

"I said go back to bed."

Carl heard the rush of something falling, more like slipping away. Something fragile, light. He turned.

She had let her nightgown slip off her. She stood there buck naked, facing him.

Now, Polly was no spring chicken, but she'd had a fair amount of work done to her. Her breasts were small, though no longer saggy.

Her hips were thin, and her recently waxed legs belonged to a younger woman. She did her best to look directly at Carl. That wasn't easy given the residue of booze coursing through her veins.

The expression on Carl's face crushed her. At her deposition she had described her husband's reaction as pure revulsion.

Carl left the room and went to their bedroom. After a while Polly picked up her nightgown and followed.

Carl had locked the bedroom door.

I remember that night at Diane's, looking across the East River at that one building that stuck out, dwarfing the rest of the Manhattan skyline, wondering, *Who lives there?*

Carl made some important decisions that night. Those that dealt with Dunn & Sullivan would affect a lot of people. Me very much among them.

His other decision was to move out of his apartment the next day. He started living with someone he'd been seeing on and off for some time. A fitness instructor, quite attractive, with a near-perfect body, though not too bright.

His name was William Cunningham.

And he, too, was about to play a role in all this.

9.

I filed the asset-seizure case on Wednesday close of business, the day before Thanksgiving.

I wanted to catch GRE's lawyers off guard. Make responding more burdensome, since now they would need to prepare their opposition papers during Thanksgiving and the run-up to Christmas, typically a downtime for litigation.

That was the way the game was played. Big Law took advantage of any opportunity to inflict pain on the other side. That's how I was trained. That's what you did.

You know, lawyering isn't nurtured by genius. No, the mother's milk of lawyering is preparation.

You worked thousands of hours, reading, rereading, researching, and drafting memos and position papers and legal pleadings, over and over and over. Logging billable hour upon billable hour upon billable hour. You sat at your desk, at your computer. Writing. Reading. Thinking. Day and night.

You took advantage of any opportunity to blindside your adversary, just as your adversary sought to do with you. So long as what you did was professionally ethical and not in violation of the prescribed rules of the road that lawyers were required to follow . . . well, you did what you needed to do.

My focus back then was on that road. On being a team player.

I should have looked in the rearview mirror once in a while.

I did learn that the Indian lawyer who'd brought the case to Dunn & Sullivan was named Dipak Singh. We didn't meet until later— more about that soon—but did speak briefly by phone. He was polite, lightly accented. And uninformative.

In our papers filed with the New York federal court, we asked that GRE's response time be shortened, claiming urgency, a need to seize assets before the company could sell or otherwise dispose of them.

I didn't know then which law firm represented GRE. I hadn't met Peter Moss. Knew nothing about him.

But I would.

10.

Thanksgiving was at the Hell's Kitchen apartment. It was something.

Even though it was a holiday, I went to the office on Thursday and stayed too long.

I got to the apartment just as my dad, Rosy, and Sean were sitting down to dinner. It was traditional turkey and trimmings. Rosy was a terrible cook, but she did manage to make what looked like the meal you'd expect to see on Thanksgiving.

Just as I reached the landing at the top of the third flight, Rosy opened the door. I got the big hug. The double cheek kiss.

"You're here," Rosy said, holding on to me tight.

"Hey, sweetie," I said. Rosy smelled like whiskey.

Once she let go and I got a better look I could see there was more than booze going on. (Or should I say going *in*?) While I didn't know it at the time, she and Sean were already signed on to a serious crystal-meth habit.

Sean and my dad had just seated themselves at the dining table. I hung my coat in the entranceway closet and joined them. Sean got up. My father didn't.

I hugged Sean.

"Bro," he said, slapping my back. "Glad you could make it."

I gave him my *What can you do?* look. Then I went over to my dad.

"Hey, Dad," I said, bending to hug him. He just sat there.

"You're late, boy," he said. To Dad I am—and have always been—"boy."

I let it go and took my seat.

Sean started to carve the turkey. He was standing at the table in one of his marine *semper fi* T-shirts (these old New York apartments are always overheated). My brother's tattooed muscles were bulging, but his hands were shaking.

"Want me to do the honors?" I asked, thinking Sean was about to carve himself rather than that undernourished bird lying on the chipped serving plate.

"Got it, bro," Sean said. "No worries."

And then he sliced into his thumb.

"Shit! Goddamn it!" he said, dropping the carving knife on the table and grabbing his hand.

Rosy got some super-strength Band-Aids from the bathroom cabinet and wrapped them tightly around Sean's thumb. Back in his chair now, he held his bandaged hand up like a sixth-grader asking his teacher if he could go use the bathroom.

"You okay?" I asked.

"Fucking A-OK," Sean said, his eyes crinkly, grinning.

Sean of course was also drunk. Or stoned. Or both.

"You need to be more careful, lad," my father told Sean.

Sean was always "lad" to my "boy."

My dad then rose from his seat. He reached over for the carving knife. I watched as he fumbled across the table. Almost too sloshed to stand. With my dad that was hardly a shocker, since he was shitfaced most of the time. For a minute it looked like he was about to tumble right onto the turkey.

I half stood to get the carving knife ahead of him.

"Here, let me do it," I told my father.

That caused my father to reach farther and harder. He stumbled and almost upended the table, but he did manage to grab the knife.

"You'll do no such thing," my dad said. "I will carve."

And somehow he did.

I can remember my father as a younger man. My memories begin with him coming though the door after work, tall and thin, once in a while still in his doorman's uniform. He looked weirdly like some army big shot with the visored cap and the epaulets on his greatcoat.

My mother was always there to greet him. She'd help him off with his coat and hang it in the entranceway closet. And while she was doing this, she would take soundings.

What sort of mood was my old man in? Or, to put it more succinctly, how bad a mood was he in?

Dad would ignore his boys and go directly to the fridge for a beer. The whiskey from the cabinet in the living room would follow in short order.

Mom would always feed Sean and me before my dad got home. For years I thought that was just the way it was in families. I didn't understand until later that our mom was protecting us from him. Sometimes Dad would drink himself unconscious at the table. He'd slump over, and our mother would then get him up and guide him into their bedroom.

And then there were the other nights.

The old man would look at his sons. Watching. Like a house cat with a cornered mouse. And we'd wait, frozen, knowing that something was coming. Just what? And how bad this time?

Well, there was no predicting. Like I said, Mom ran as much interference as she could. I also didn't understand until much later that my dad was afraid of Sean. Sean would take my dad's abuse. But only up to a point. When he'd had enough, he'd let Dad know. Not with words. Just a look telling the old man, *Enough*. And drunk as he was, Dad would back off.

Then, the next morning at work, there would be our dad, at his station in the Park Avenue co-op's lobby, smiling and gently joking with the residents. Tousling the hair of the little tykes being led out to a waiting car by their mothers or nannies. Gentle Irish Seamus Blake in his general's uniform and his lovely, lilting, Gaelic way of speaking.

Like a lot of people who have had alcoholic parents and siblings, I drink, too, but watchfully. People like us have seen what booze can do to a person.

Rosy had placed a bottle of red wine on the table. That was meant for me. This was emphatically not a wine-drinking family. Sean was chugalugging Pabst from the can. Dad and Rosy were deep into the Jameson's, the two-thirds-gone Irish whiskey standing sentry next to the untouched red. Rosy must have gotten some assistance from the liquor store, because that wine was an "in the know" Napa cabernet (like she'd seen me order at Keens) that must have put her back fifty or sixty bucks. Maybe even more. How could you not love Rosy and her big heart?

I took some of the red, poured it into the juice glass that Rosy had set out. (Wine goblets in this family?) Then we all started eating, each of us forking or spooning from the serving plates in the middle of the table. (And Rosy's cooking was truly awful.)

"So," my dad said after a while.

I didn't look up from my plate. Didn't have to. I knew the drill. As they say: been there, done that.

"So," he repeated, waiting for his dutiful son to face him.

Then I did.

A pause, Dad eyeing me, and then, "How's life among the swells?"

"Fine."

As self-conscious as it was, I went back head-down to my greasy turkey, bracing myself for the oncoming barrage. (How is it we become involuntary children around our parents?)

"Haven't forgotten where you came from, have ya, boy?"

Big brother to the rescue.

"How could anyone ever forget that?" Sean told our dad, grandly motioning around the room. "Lap o' luxury we came from? Huh, Dad?"

My father ignored Sean. He was coming after me.

He reached for and grabbed the red wine bottle and ostentatiously studied the label. He stuck out his jaw, nodded his head. Signaling, I guess, something like, *Fancy wine for my fancy son.* We all watched as he replaced the bottle back to where it had been.

"So tell us all what life is like these days among your betters."

My betters?

He was getting to me. Every word or phrase loaded with the history of being his son, of enduring years of this. I was eight-year-old Carney Blake again. How could I still fall for this shit?

Sean and I exchanged glances. Drunk or stoned as he was, he was signaling me: *Cool down, bro. The guy's an asshole. You know that.*

"It's fine."

I was mumbling, angry with myself for slipping so quickly back into childhood, yet unable not to.

That brought a smirk from my father. He was just getting started.

"And you're now a partner in that fancy law company you work for?"

Only a nod this time.

Then my dad's nodding, too, jaw stuck out. Just like he'd done with the wine bottle.

"And tell me, boy, are these grandees you're workin' for inviting you to their homes now? Introducin' you to their daughters?"

"Carney's got a nice girlfriend."

This time it was Rosy to the rescue.

"Do tell," my dad said to Rosy. And then to me.

"So who is this lucky lass?"

Rosy again.

"She's a lawyer, just like Carney."

"A lawyer? Well, then."

Dad nodding, feigning admiration. His eyes narrowing, all the while preparing his next barb. The drunk son of a bitch.

When not in his presence, I could calmly tell you that what my father was doing was projecting onto me his own sense of inadequacy, his own deep frustrations at how his miserable, mediocre life turned out. But in his presence? It was like a knife between the ribs.

"And you've met her, then?" Dad said to Rosy. Turning on her. About to stick that knife in her.

And that, my brother was not about to allow.

"Yeah, Dad," Sean interjected. "We both have. The girl's a beaut. Black Irish, Dad. I mean *really* black Irish."

With that came the Sean Blake grin, his mirthful-eyed instant-messaging system. My father could see something was up. Wasn't as it should be. Something he wasn't going to be at all happy with.

Then he got it. "Tell me, boy," aimed directly at me.

"Tell you what?"

"You aren't, are you?"

"Aren't what, Dad?"

"A Negress?"

"A what?"

"There'll be no black bitches in my house. At my table."

His house? His table? I pay the rent on this shitty little apartment. That's it. I was done. I pulled the paper napkin off my lap, about to get to my feet and get the hell out of there.

Before I had the chance, my father stuck his fork in a big chunk of turkey thigh from the serving dish and dropped it onto my plate.

"This'll be the only dark meat that's ever gonna be at my table. Ya got that, boy?"

I was stunned. Didn't utter a word.

"Go on, boy," he said. "Eat up."

While this was going on, Sean had risen from the table and disappeared. I hardly noticed at the time. And then, just as my father was taunting me with his "dark meat" insult, Sean returned.

He had gone to the bedroom that he and Rosy slept in, the room that I had shared with him when we were kids. He calmly walked up to the table. In his hand was his .45-caliber semiautomatic. Fully loaded.

Sean stood there facing my seated father. He lifted the pistol, then racked a shell into the chamber. Sean placed the gun on the table to the right of his plate and sat down.

"Now, Dad," he said. "That'll be enough. You're gonna need to behave. Or at least shut the fuck up if you can't say something nice. You can do that, can't you, Dad?"

Nothing from our father. He was stunned like the rest of us.

Sean then slammed his fist on the table hard enough to rattle the dishes.

"Gonna need a response here, Dad."

I saw my father's eyes darken, saw something primeval, murderous. He was raging inside. Drunk. Angry. And now humiliated.

Rosy's eyes were darting back and forth, first to Sean, then my dad, then me, then back to Sean. My father clenched his fists. Started to rise.

No one said a word.

And then surrender bled into his eyes. His pickled brain shut down. You could actually see it happening.

He mumbled something about needing to go to the bathroom, managed to get himself up from the table, and staggered toward the back of the apartment.

We watched him go. The food on our plates now untouched, cold. Sean and me sitting there in the shadow of the old man.

Just like always.

But this was no longer my life. Just a bad night.

Thank the good Lord, I silently told myself (like my mother would have said). For me things were looking up. I had been placed in charge of an interesting new case. My first one. I was long gone from Hell's Kitchen, making more money than I needed. And I had a new girlfriend. Not bad for a kid from this neighborhood.

So a few minutes later, there I was outside on Eighth Avenue, huddled back in my topcoat, frost on my breath, hailing an uptown cab to my Sixty-second Street apartment.

As the driver did the potholed New York version of the Indianapolis 500, I bounced around in the back watching the blocks fly by and thanking my lucky stars.

And then a few weeks later, on Christmas Eve, I was served with GRE's motions to dismiss our asset-seizure case.

I began reading.

My first thought?

Give me a break.

11.

By 6:30 p.m. the office had cleared out.

Not another lawyer in sight. Like I said, it was Christmas Eve.

So it was just me and the nighttime all-Hispanic cleaning crew, some sporting white-fringed red Santa caps, others curiously wearing paper Burger King crowns.

They were in a seasonally jovial mood, wishing me a *"Feliz Navidad"* each time they passed my open door.

I was sitting there, glued to GRE's pleading. It had been filed with the federal court literally minutes before its clerk's office closed for the day. (Like I said earlier, that's how the game was played.) Courtesy copies had also been messengered to Dunn & Sullivan by opposing counsel as required.

I had to leave. Should have by now. Diane had invited me for Christmas Eve dinner, and I was already late. She was staying in New York for Christmas. Because of me. (I'd told her about my Thanksgiving.)

GRE's lawyers had leveled some really nasty charges. It looked to me like a smoke-screen defense. They weren't trying to justify what they did in India. Like they say, the best defense is a good offense.

Or like that old lawyer's adage:

If you're weak on the law, pound the facts. If you're weak on the facts, pound the law. And if you're weak on both the facts and the law, pound the table.

Meaning go after the other side. Get personal. Nasty. Dirty.

And so what were these charges?

A supposed comprehensive scheme to (1) bribe the Indian judge with expensive gifts, (2) ghostwrite the "independent" expert-witness reports relied on by the judge, and (3) ghostwrite the judge's opinion itself, allowing the judge to then pawn it off as his own handiwork.

But you know, the more I read, the more I thought about it, the more I began to think, could there be . . . ?

Whoa, I told myself. *Get a grip. Slow down. You're an advocate. You have a side to protect. You're a litigation partner in a major American law firm. Not some wet-behind-the-ears kid lawyer whose knees buckle the minute the other side throws some punches your way.* I was a made man. (Well, okay, maybe the Mafia metaphor was pushing it.)

I laid the pleading back on my desk, swiveled my chair to the window behind, and looked down at the Times Square night, dazzlingly lit, teeming with throngs of people and cars.

"Feliz Navidad, señor."

Standing in my open doorway were two young women from the cleaning crew. Early twenties at the most. Both were short, a little stocky, with pretty, angelic faces. And wearing Burger King crowns.

I'm sure I had passed these two countless other evenings when they were heads-down in the hallway, going about their after-hours minimum-wage chores. Invisible. Tonight they were smiling, filled with Christmas spirit.

"Mismo a usted," I said in my best high-school Spanish.

They giggled. Pleased, I guess, to get a response in their own language from an American *abogado*.

We waved at each other, and then they moved on, the second in line lugging an industrial-size vacuum cleaner half as big as she was.

I retook my seat and once again picked up the GRE pleading.

Look. It was just a pleading. Just allegations. Proof of nothing. Not a word about what actually happened at the time of the plant explosion. Not one word trying to justify what GRE's management did, or tried to do, to ensure the safety of its workers. Only these scurrilous charges about how the case had been tried.

I knew full well that lawyers are given certain leeway to write things in pleadings that may not—let us say—be truly factworthy. Not technically lies, but assertions following time-tested lawyer "wiggle words" like "on information and belief," so-and-so did this or that.

Those wiggle words give lawyers a degree of immunity. Like an ethical get-out-of-jail-free card, allowing them to make claims that won't necessarily hold up in court. And when that happens?

The lawyer tells the judge, "Look, that's what the client told me happened. Remember, I didn't say I knew, I said 'on information and belief.' It's not on me. I promise I did what I could to verify. How was I supposed to know? I'm just the lawyer. My job is to advocate, and that's what I tried my darnedest to do."

Then the client loses his/her case. The lawyer pockets his/her fee. The client goes home empty-handed. The lawyer moves on to the next client.

And the words "on information and belief" were sprinkled over GRE's allegations like cracked pepper over a dinner-size Caesar salad.

And no way would someone like Carl Smith allow a case into his law firm that was tainted in the way the pleadings said this one was.

No way.

That's what I was thinking.

12.

Late again by the time I left our building.

I jogged down the entrance to the Forty-second Street subway station and impatiently waited on the platform for a train to Queens. The trains were on a holiday schedule, so I had a long wait. Finally the 7 train pulled up. I took it to Vernon-Jackson. Raced along the platform to the station exit, leaped the steps two at a time, and beelined it to Diane's building at 4610 Center Boulevard, right behind that big outdoor "Pepsi" sign on the promenade that's been there for I don't know how long. By the time I arrived, I was bathed in sweat, wrapped as I was in suit, tie, and topcoat.

I raced through the lobby of her building, not giving the doorman behind the counter time to stop me and ask which resident I was visiting. There were no shouts from him as I turned the corner for the bank of elevators. Maybe he recognized me from earlier visits?

Willing the elevator to speed up, I got off at Diane's floor, and then it hit me. I was supposed to bring wine. "Shit," I murmured as I ferociously thrust my arm into the almost closed elevator doors.

Then it was down to the lobby and out the door so I could run back up to the 4700 block of Center Boulevard, where there was a wine shop.

Quick purchase, grabbing a white from the cooler and a red from the racks. Credit card. Sign. Thanks very much. Return smile of young male clerk, wearing hipster clothes, sort of like what backwater farmers wear but much skinnier and tighter. And with a decidedly non-farmer haircut, slick long hair on top with buzz-cut sides. Oh, and colorful, strategically placed tattoos on forearms and neck.

Back through the lobby. Elevator. Come on, come on.

And then at Diane's. Hello kiss. Apology for lateness. Coat, suit jacket, and tie off. Open top collar button. Express delight over kitchen smells. Sit down to dinner, now on verge of being overcooked.

And then.

"What's wrong?"

We had been sitting across from each other at the small blond table pressed up against the oversize window looking out over the Manhattan skyline. The view was nothing short of spectacular. Manhattan's landmark buildings (Empire State, Chrysler, and so on) were lit in blazing red and green.

Christmastime in New York.

Well, wrapped in my thoughts as I was, there could have been a massive, belching New Jersey refinery out there and I wouldn't have noticed.

Diane had roasted a turkey. (For me, not her.) It was the missing twin of the one that Rosy had cremated. Miraculously *not* overcooked by my lateness. This one was succulent, tender, juicy, and accompanied by an array of sides all hand-selected by Diane from a nearby farmers' market held each Saturday morning at an otherwise vacant lot over on Forty-eighth Avenue and Vernon Boulevard.

In other words, Diane had gone all out here, had spent considerable time and effort making this dinner for me. And she had chosen to miss her family's Lake Charles Christmas.

And I was behaving like some petulant child, sulking because some other kid on the playground had called me and my friends a bunch of names.

I must not have heard Diane the first time.

"I said what's wrong?"

"Huh?"

I was miles away.

"All good," I then managed, with a politician's sincerity. Adding in the same unhelpful voice, "Great dinner."

Then I beamed back up to my starship.

And that's pretty much how our dinner went. There was some perfunctory conversation. Must have been, since we sat across from each other and ate.

I drank too much wine. So much for the child of alcoholics' booze awareness.

When we finished dinner, we both started cleaning up. We were at the sink in Diane's kitchen area. She was rinsing, and I was stacking the dishwasher, still light-years away. Diane saw that.

She shut off the water and turned to me. We stood facing each other. Close. Diane took my hand and then led me to the bedroom. I looked back at the sink and counter, still piled with dishes, glasses, and whatnot. Diane shook her head, silently telling me, *Leave it.*

The only light in her bedroom came from what crept in through the open doorway. But it was enough. Again we stood facing each other. Diane started kissing me, unbuttoning my shirt. Then she took my face in both her hands, moved me eye to eye with her.

"Baby," she whispered. "It's a job. That's all. Not life or death."

And then Diane pressed her lips to mine. Those succulent lips. We kissed long and hard. Whatever perfume she had on was working. That and the potent aroma of her warm presence so close to me. When we finally separated, we undressed and got into bed.

. . .

After we finished, I fell dead asleep. I awoke hours later, slipped out of bed, and returned to the kitchen. When I flipped on the lights, I saw that Diane had already been out here and cleaned up.

I returned to the bedroom. Back in bed, I spooned into Diane. She slid in closer.

Now awake. Thinking. To find a woman like this? That's a Christmas gift.

All true.

Still. Those pleadings.

It was a job. But not *just* a job. I was a lawyer. I had a sworn duty to my clients. I'm not going to get all operatic about it. But it wasn't just a job.

Not life or death, she had said.

Well . . .

13.

I could see him, but I couldn't hear him.

A guy playing a saxophone on the sidewalk forty-five floors below, directly across the street from our offices.

It was 10:00 a.m. on Monday. He had to be freezing his ass off in this blistery mid-January weather. There was an open instrument case at his feet, probably with a smattering of dollars and coins he'd put in himself to encourage passersby to toss in some of their own loose change.

The best I could tell from up here, the saxophonist looked to be in his late fifties, though he might have been older. He was wearing a long, worn-looking coat and had on one of those oversize green-and-yellow-striped Rasta knit caps. The kind for shoving your dreadlocks under. While he played, he would raise his sax and tilt his head back. As I said, I was too many floors up to hear, but it looked like he was really into it.

So Christmas was Christmas. Diane and I went with Rosy to midnight Mass. But not in the old neighborhood. I hadn't been to that church in ages. We went to St. Joseph's in the Village. Dad and Sean didn't go.

I hadn't set eyes on my father since Thanksgiving. And that was more than okay with me.

New Year's Eve we caught a movie—Diane and me, that is. After Mass, Rosy took off and more or less disappeared. I hadn't seen Sean either.

He and I did a few cell-to-cells. But it was just "brotherspeak." You know? *Hey, what's up, how's it going? . . . Good, you? . . . Yeah, all good.* Sean was keeping his distance from me. His crystal-meth habit was pulling him down. He didn't want me to see him like that.

I had been chained to my desk writing the plaintiffs' opposition brief to GRE's motion to throw out the case. I did it myself. Without help.

Big Law says that was wrong.

Why?

Leveraging. Or more accurately, the absence of leveraging.

Lawyer hourly rates at Dunn & Sullivan were steep. I won't tell you what the firm charged for my services. It's embarrassing. (Six hundred or maybe even seven hundred dollars an hour, you're thinking? Think higher.) Anyway, that's not where the real money was. For that you needed to populate cases with a full bevy of young associates and paralegals. The point was to have multiple meters running, all at the same time, as many as the case would take.

I had been assigned two juniors for this case. We younger partners couldn't simply go out into the halls and select our own helpers. We needed to requisition them like jeeps from the army motor pool. I had called the firm's staff member in charge of divvying out the juniors.

Me: I need a fourth-year associate and a paralegal for the GRE case.

Her: Just two people?

Me: Yes.

Her: That's a big case. You need more help than that.

Me: Two should do it.

Her: You need to think about that.

(*Some silence on my end.*)

Her (*again*): So . . . how many?

Me: Two. (*But I was feeling uneasy. Thinking, first, maybe I should get some more, even if I didn't really need them. Then. But just to placate her? No way.*)

Her: Okay. (*But it was one of those "okay"s with an edge to it.*)

Then I asked for the two I wanted by name. It turned out they were available. In fact, I was expecting them any minute.

So I was reading my draft pleading for the umpteenth time, still making small changes and adjustments, when I heard the knock on my door.

"Come on in," I said as I blocked and stacked the loose pages so I could have them copied and given to the two juniors I figured were out there about to come in here.

But it wasn't them.

Richard Miller ("Mad Dog") stuck his large head into my office. Other than at a distance, I hadn't seen him since he almost knocked me down when he stormed out of Carl Smith's office. There was no shortage of office scuttlebutt about him.

The younger lawyers universally considered him an equal-opportunity abuser. His rantings and ravings, and other assorted over-the-top antics, made him the butt of some razor-edged lampooning. Not that the guy didn't deserve it. Two years ago, at a private Halloween party attended by Dunn & Sullivan associates, one attendee came dressed as Mad Dog, with inflated chest and special growling Mad Dog mask he had commissioned from a Broadway costume shop. Don't know if Miller ever found out about that. The young lawyer left the firm soon thereafter, but for what reason or under what circumstances, I never found out.

Miller made a quick visual sweep of my office and saw there was only me. Then he came in and shut the door.

Just then there was a second knock. Ignoring me, he opened my door. My two juniors were standing there, here to see me as expected.

"Not now," Miller told them, and shut the door in their faces.

He came over to my desk like he owned the place. Dropped his big frame into one of my two opposite-facing chairs.

"How you doin'?" he grunted. Mad Dog was always angry at something or somebody. His right leg was motoring a mile a minute.

"Good," I said.

But I was thinking maybe I should get up and try and catch the two juniors who no doubt were walking down the hall from my office wondering what that was all about. I didn't.

As I said, Mad Dog was a senior-level partner. He had what was called a book of business, a large assortment of active legal matters that were making a meaningful presence in the firm's bottom line. A book of business brought stature. But Miller was a cheat. He padded his time and the time of those who worked for him. His expense-reimbursement requests were similarly doctored.

He had been caught on more than one occasion charging a client for personal items like tailor-made shirts, gifts for his kids, even his dry cleaning, all falsely described as client-related expenses ("supplies" or "meals" or "support assistance"). He always had an explanation: *My secretary fucked up. I grabbed the wrong goddamn form.* And so on. The time I saw him escaping from Carl Smith's office clutching that piece of paper was after another such discovery.

Carl Smith wanted Miller gone from the firm. But quietly. So he had put the word out—the way only Smith could, with no fingerprints traced back to him. Dunn & Sullivan's other lawyers should stay away from him. There was to be no working on his cases. Carl was slowly cutting off Mad Dog's oxygen supply. It would be only a matter of time, and Miller would seek employment elsewhere, his work no longer getting done.

Carl needed to avoid any scandals. Not then, on the cusp, as he was, of convincing Wall Street's bankers to take Dunn & Sullivan public. That's right. Public. What Wall Street calls an IPO—initial public offering.

Of course I didn't know it at the time, but this would be an absolute groundbreaking first for a major law firm. Going public? It had been talked about from time to time but never actually pulled off. Carl was set on pulling it off. Elevating his law firm to the ranks of GE, Westinghouse, Samsung. You name it.

It would be a transformation. No, more than that. It would be a major fucking coup. The financial press would be in a frenzy to chronicle Carl's Midas touch as he transformed the base-metal profession of lawyering into the priceless gold ingots of publicly traded stock. The market would own Dunn & Sullivan, trading its shares, and Carl's massive ownership, when transformed into stock certificates, would catapult him into the stratosphere of the mega-rich. Carl Smith. Tycoon. And, that was Carl's exit strategy.

No, a scandal was the last thing Carl needed.

"Yeah, so . . ." Miller said.

His large rib cage straining his shirt buttons, his walrus mustache, those blue-tinted steel-rimmed glasses, the widow's-peak receding hairline, even the way he sat forward—all of it telegraphed an unmistakable menace.

Here it comes, I told myself, bracing for impact.

". . . I need you on some of my work. Effective immediately."

I didn't say anything. My mind was in overdrive, searching for the exit ramp that would allow me to veer away from this guy.

Miller was reciting a long list of tasks and projects he wanted done. And then . . .

"Are you paying attention here? Pick up your goddamn pen and start taking notes."

"Yeah, well," I said. "Here's the thing . . ."

That's as far as I got.

"Here's the fucking *what*?"

"Richard, I'm actually immersed in a case that Carl Smith has assigned to me."

I stopped there, thinking how could I say what I was about to say without pushing down the plunger on the dynamite detonator?

Turns out I already had.

Mad Dog sprang to his feet. He stormed around the side of my desk. Towering over me, he aimed his index finger at my sternum.

"You do not tell a senior partner of this law firm that you are too busy for an assignment. You got that?"

I swallowed my instinct. The one telling me to stand up and ram this asshole's head through my far wall. That was another life. A long time ago. That was no longer me.

Miller was waiting for a response.

"Okay."

Miller nodded once, apparently now satisfied, then abruptly turned and headed for my door. Over his shoulder he told me that he'd have the files sent to me immediately, adding:

"And get associate help. You're gonna need it."

And then he was gone.

I stayed seated. More shaken than relieved. Second-guessing myself for so easily capitulating.

This wasn't just a moment of weakness, my unconditional surrender.

I wanted to fit in here, even though I think I knew deep down that someone like me doesn't. Not really. As I said, I considered myself the consummate team player. I wanted this. I got it. I wanted to keep it.

Other than perhaps being a judge, a lawyer like me can't do better than being a partner in one of the country's best law firms. I told myself it wasn't the money. Or the stature. But was I kidding myself?

Was this what my father's taunt was about? Carney Blake among his betters? While I didn't think of them as my betters, was his message right for all the wrong reasons? That I didn't belong and maybe I was trying too hard to do just that?

I turned to my window (I'd been doing that a lot lately) and looked back down at the saxophonist, still there, still silently playing music.

Watching him, I felt like I was deaf.

And when I think back on that time, I was blind as well.

14.

"Good shot, Senator."

Actually, the shooter was a congressman. But that was of no concern to the hunting guide who had also fired at the flock of geese fooled into landing near a clump of strategically placed decoys. So far as he was concerned, the guy was just another muckety-muck. He called them all Senator.

And it had been the guide's shot that had struck that unfortunate and apparently nearsighted bird, now lying belly-up among its plastic replicas in the final twitching throes of a death spiral. The congressman's shot had gone wild. The guide's job was to ensure that the lawmaker took credit for the kill.

The congressman high-fived the day's other public official, another congressman, though of the opposite political party, absolutely ecstatic with his nonexistent marksmanship.

"How about that?" he exclaimed to his legislative colleague, bouncing on his feet with the excitement of a teenager in front of his first car. "Bring 'em on," he then told the guide, standing stone-faced beside him.

The congressman and his colleague were both outfitted in head-to-toe unsullied, laundry-pressed camo, immaculate versions of what the others in the hunting blind were wearing. They were both in their sixties, portly and jowled, unwitting specimens of the overindulged life furtively enjoyed by so many of those whose hot air got them elected to Congress.

They were guests of Peter Moss and his law firm, the host for the day's outing. Peter had organized the shooting and for the first time had included his fifteen-year-old son, Josh, still on Christmas break from his boarding school.

Actually, the real host, at least in terms of paying for the hunting, the eating and drinking, the rooms from the night before, possibly even an honorarium for each of the congressmen if they would accept one, was the last participant in this hunt. It was his blind, his farm, and his money.

The guy was the CEO of a natural-gas-exploration company that was into "fracking" U.S. lands—a deep drilling process that injected fluids laden with carcinogenic and otherwise toxic chemicals under extreme high pressure deep into the earth's surface to fracture rocks and release trapped gas.

His company was Peter Moss's client. Trouble was brewing for this industry on Capitol Hill. Peter's job was to crush the newly proposed regulatory scheme designed to protect the environment by limiting—or, heaven forbid, shutting down—all future fracking on public lands. Even if it was causing sinkholes and earthquakes from the subterranean pocket voids where the gas had been.

The two congressmen were members of the House energy subcommittee that had oversight over the fracking industry. Under House rules they could socialize with civilians (lawyers, lobbyists, corporate fat cats), but they were required to pay for their own meals and lodging. And these two did. But only at a fraction of the cost of what the hunting party would spend on this outing.

Peter's law firm would pick up the bill, pay for everything, and then charge a tiny part of it to each congressman as his "share" of the festivities. Peter would then lay off the full charge to the client.

This client was only too happy to pay for the outing, no matter the cost. The same was true when Peter would present his outsize legal bill, stating only "for services rendered" with no further detail.

While it was certainly true that corporate America was tightening its belt when it came to paying legal fees, this was different. The exception that proved the rule. There would be no team of young lawyers toiling for hours over documents, no midnight-oil legal research, no multidraft court pleadings. No ticking time clocks. None of that was needed.

Sometime after this weekend's shooting festivities, Peter would make a trip, alone, up to Capitol Hill. A whisper in the ears of a couple of congressmen, then with a collective bipartisan stroke of the pen a troublesome law would be changed. And that was that.

And while never a word was spoken, both congressmen knew that a job would most likely be waiting for them at Peter's law firm should they ever actually lose an election. Former members of Congress had priority access through Washington's revolving door.

The "farm," a manicured estate dating back to Revolutionary times, was located on Maryland's famed Eastern Shore, the flatlands surrounding the vast Chesapeake Bay, roughly an hour and a half's drive from Washington, D.C. The area was a mecca for waterfowl shooting, situated as it was directly under the flight path of Canada's migratory goose and duck populations.

"Get down. Get down."

That was the guide again. His trained ears had picked up the sound of the next incoming flock.

Peter carefully peered over the blind's concealing shrubbery and saw the vector of incoming geese. Still high, out of range, but heading this way.

He placed his hand on Josh's shoulder and gently guided him to the required crouching position. He held his forefinger to his lips, letting his son know that this was the crucial time, that absolute silence was necessary as the guide attempted to call in the still-high-flying birds, closer now, having spotted the decoys and provisionally interested. The guide was using one of his six-inch cylindrical wooden goose callers that he kept tied around his neck with rawhide strips. This was a delicate process. It required absolute stillness in the blind. Even the two congressmen shut up for once.

"Grab your gun," Peter whispered to Josh, watching as he did so, making sure the boy left the safety on until ready, as he'd been taught.

Crouched in this blind, keeping a watchful eye on his son, Peter Moss was practicing law.

As far as Peter was concerned, lawyering was made up of a mix of ingredients. Like a potent drink. Understanding the law, knowing how to use the law, how to argue it when necessary—all were part of the mix. So were assertiveness, aggression, creativity. Put all that into a cocktail shaker. Add a splash of deviousness. Shake and pour. There you go.

To Peter, putting those two congressmen in that goose blind was actually the essence of lawyering. So was the way he had positioned the GRE case, something he thought of more as an offensive weapon than a lawsuit.

Days after GRE had hired Moss and his law firm to defend it against asset seizures, Peter had contacted Dipak Singh. He had invited his adversary to Washington, hinting at a settlement. The prospect of flipping the Indian judgment into quick money put Dipak on a plane. Remember, he was dangerously low on funds. And while he might have been lured to Washington under false pretenses, there would be something in this for him.

Peter Moss wanted Dipak to hire Dunn & Sullivan as the plaintiffs' lawyers. In fact, he would pay Dipak handsomely (under the table, as I said) to do just that.

How did Dipak react to this unorthodox request from his client's adversary for him to have his own American counsel handpicked? *By the opposition?* He didn't give it a moment's thought. The prospect of cash in his pocket turned him into Helen Keller.

Keep in mind Dipak had a good case. His clients were indeed grievously injured by the negligence and disregard of GRE. To win his case in India, he had to do what he had to do. No choice, really. Though to him it came quite easily. It was in his bones given his family's long history of acquired stature in a society that often too easily condoned crooked paths. Right and wrong were relative concepts to this young lawyer. And despite his outward appearance, Dipak was no legal eagle.

He would be paid by the enemy to handpick counsel for his own side? Fine. Keep it a secret? Also fine.

And Peter Moss, for his part, would make a handsome fee on his defense of GRE for his law firm. But there was more.

Handing off the prosecution of this polluted case to Dunn & Sullivan—knowing Carl Smith as he did—was indeed a monkey trap, but it was something more as well. The coconut was a time bomb.

Sooner or later that bomb would explode, and if Peter's timing was on target, he would have a damaged Dunn & Sullivan in his crosshairs, like some wounded waterfowl, hobbled and ready for the kill. "Kill" in this case meaning Peter's hostile takeover of whatever parts of Dunn & Sullivan he wanted to absorb into his own law firm.

And speaking of wounded birds.

"Now!" the guide shouted as those in the blind rose, shotguns at the ready, and opened fire at the flock of lowering geese, all of whom were desperately trying to reverse course and get the hell out of there.

Both congressmen's shots went wild. The guide squeezed off two quick rounds, one dead bird for each of them. Peter didn't fire and instead kept watch on his son, whose shot struck a bird but off center, the buckshot obliterating one of its wings. The bird fell to earth smack in the middle of the decoys. It righted itself, trying to fly off, and when that wasn't possible, it frantically tried scampering away, repeatedly stumbling, then righting itself, then stumbling again.

One of the foremost rules of waterfowl hunting was that wounded prey must be caught and put out of their misery.

This was Peter's son's bird. It was his job to deal with it.

"Let's go, Josh," Peter told the boy as he guided him out of the blind and onto the decoy field and the wounded goose.

Peter's son was hesitant. He stood watching the crippled goose's wild and frenzied escape attempt. He turned to his father.

"Dad?" was all he said, but his meaning was clear enough. *Do I have to?*

"Go," Peter told him. "Get him, Josh."

Shooting a wounded bird at point-blank range was considered unsportsmanlike. Peter's son would need to kill the bird with his bare hands.

Each time Josh managed to get near the goose, it would right itself and scamper away, its eyes displaying the abject terror it instinctively felt. Josh would chase the goose, the goose would again right itself, lurch, and wobble a few feet away before again collapsing.

"Get 'em, boy!" the guide yelled from the blind. This being the first bit of real entertainment of the day for him.

After three or four more tries, Josh managed to grab the goose by its long neck. He held the bird out at arm's length, his eyes showing as much fear as the bird's. Peter caught up to him.

"Wring his neck," he told the boy. "Just swing the bird around a couple of wide arcs until it's dead. Go on. The bird is suffering. Do it."

But he couldn't. Josh stood with the squirming, bloody bird in his hands, his eyes welling with tears. He just couldn't do it.

"Here," Peter told Josh as he grabbed the bird. He then swirled the bird a few times around until he was certain its neck was broken. He then led his son back to the blind, dropping the goose carcass on the ground just outside the entrance. Before Josh stepped back into the blind, he turned to face his father.

"Dad, I'm . . ." he said, trying as best he could to hold back tears.

"It's okay, Joshie," was all Peter said as he turned his boy and guided him back into the blind.

And what was *Peter* feeling?

Like so many men and women who defined themselves by their careers, there wasn't much to Peter Moss other than his work. *A man is what he does.*

Moss would say that he loved his wife. And he thought he did, though he never dwelled on it. When it came to his son, that love was more intrinsic. Rooted. Peter's love for Josh was genuinely paternal. No question about it. But the essence of Peter— his unassailable self-image—required *this* son someday to become *this* father. It was a sort of reverse narcissism. And Josh just didn't seem wired for the job.

As he followed his son back into the blind, this simple episode, Josh's excruciating discomfort with this blood sport, told Peter something. To do what Peter Moss did, you needed to be a killer—not actually, of course, but in the vocational way that society accepts. To him that was the essence of advocacy.

Josh could very well someday become a lawyer, just not one like his father. Peter admired and emulated the lawyers who *drove* the buses; the rest were just passengers along for the ride.

This boy was going to disappoint him.

So be it, Peter thought.

But that thought wouldn't take. Despite his love for his son, Peter simply couldn't help relegating Josh to some lesser role in the world's order.

How sad.

15.

While I was staring out my window lost in thought, and while Peter Moss was "practicing law" out in the goose blind, Carl Smith was sunning himself.

This was Carl's last day at his Naples, Florida, home, here for the holidays without his wife, though not alone. He had just gotten off the phone with the New York investment bankers responsible for underwriting the Dunn & Sullivan IPO.

Carl slid his iPhone under a towel on the small table beside his chaise lounge. It was late morning and already too hot to leave it directly in the sun. He reapplied sunscreen over his tan though skeletal body, pasting his motley collection of graying hairs to his bony chest, then rubbing the cream onto his essentially hairless legs.

He grabbed his sunglasses from the side table and watched William Cunningham as he worked out on the poolside equipment Carl had bought for him: a bench press, a lat machine, an assortment of free weights. William had a big, blond, hairy chest and muscular arms and legs. *Nice*, Carl thought as he watched his young lover go through his routine.

Each morning since the two of them had come down here, William would slip out of bed just after dawn, careful not to wake Carl, and go out for his nine- or ten-mile run. Later in the morning, as Carl hung by the pool, either on the phone or reading documents, William would lift weights. Carl hadn't so much as put a toe in the water, either in his pool or in the ocean of this waterfront home.

While he couldn't convince Carl to run, or even walk, with him in the early mornings, William knew that Carl liked watching him exercise. He could sometimes see the growing bulge in Carl's swim trunks. That's why he went out of his way to flex between reps; it turned Carl on, and William liked that—it made for better sex in the afternoon when they both went indoors to escape the noonday sun. It also made for a more generous Carl when they went shopping later in the day.

So, all in all, William played and Carl worked.

Carl was tracking the investment bank's due diligence on the IPO. He was pleased with their progress. And he was proud of himself for having so effectively beefed up Dunn & Sullivan's balance sheet with the five or six plaintiffs' contingent-fee cases he'd brought in, each with the mostly illusory promise of off-the-chart legal fees.

It was a clever plan, bringing these cases of questionable value into Dunn & Sullivan. There was some chance of success for them, though at best they were long shots. They looked good on paper—if you didn't look too closely—with their expectation of big-money settlements or jury awards. And they brought immediate cash into the law firm with their hedge-fund litigation-finance loans. But the odds were stacked against them. They were probable losers.

Carl didn't care. These plaintiffs' cases added (deceptive) value to the law firm. That was good for the IPO. The higher the firm's value, the higher its stock value at the time of the initial offering to the investing public. And by that time Carl planned to be long gone with a treasure trove of stock in his name, all of it sold on the open market at the highest IPO price. By the time things at Dunn & Sullivan turned south—if they ever did—Carl Smith would be history.

Peter Moss was unaware of the upcoming IPO. (At least then he was.) So Carl Smith didn't know the GRE case was a trap (monkey or booby, take your pick), and Peter Moss didn't know of the pending public offering. Whichever happened first would surely affect the other.

Tomorrow, after returning to New York, Carl had some "domestic" business to attend to. He needed to deal with Polly. She was getting in his way. He had moved her out of the apartment, cut off her use of all but one credit card, barred her from the Naples home and the Aspen condo. Carl didn't for a moment think he was being totally heartless. For Christ's sake, he thought, hadn't he actually had her moved into a one-bedroom apartment in a still-somewhat-fashionable Upper East Side co-op?

He told her she didn't need a lawyer. Said it wasn't necessary. And what does she do? Goes and hires one of New York's most visible and vicious divorce attorneys. A guy the tabloids loved to cover, with his roster of athletes, hip-hop artists, and other newsworthy clients.

Her lawyer had called. Demanded a meeting. And he got one. At Dunn & Sullivan right before Christmas. This brainy and resourceful attorney who had the audacity to march into Carl's law firm holding Polly by the arm like she was some kind of frail and damaged little bird.

Carl took the meeting in one of the rooms in the firm's conference center, an entire floor devoted to gatherings with outside parties. The last thing he needed was his wife and her divorce lawyer walking down the hall to his corner office a few floors above.

Polly was drunk. He saw it immediately, even before he pointed her and her lawyer to seats across from him at the highly polished rectangular table. He had told the staff not to bring in coffee and other beverages, as was the norm for meetings held at the conference center. There would be no legal pads stacked on the table, no assortment of pens bearing the firm's name. Nothing. Just Carl.

Polly's lawyer was Iván Escobar, known as "Iván the Impaler" for his cutthroat tactics, his take-no-prisoners behavior. (How we lawyers love to come up with colorful or malicious monikers.)

Iván was slick and smooth, artful and nimble. There was never a shine off his shaved head, the rumor being that he retained his own private makeup artist, especially for his cameo appearances on CNN when he was called upon to opine on the latest celebrity marriage on the rocks. He was highly tailored, though not in the Carl Smith mode. No understated, elegant Brioni suits for Iván. He went to tightly fitted and boldly chalked pin-striped suits adorned with shiny silk pocket hankies, ultra-high-collared monogrammed French-cuffed shirts, and thickly knotted Countess Mara neckties. To top off the look, he wore his trademark black-rimmed, perfectly round eyeglasses.

Iván stayed in shape, so while on the short side he still made an imposing appearance. Here was a lawyer who would cut his opponent's heart out and eat it in front of him.

Incensed as Carl was over Polly's selection of counsel, he knew that Iván Escobar was not one to trifle with. All the same, he was Carl Smith, no match for some sleazeball divorce lawyer, no matter how famous and sharp he might be.

Carl stared at Escobar. Waiting. Purposefully injecting tension into the room.

"Carl . . ." Polly started to say before Escobar placed his hand over hers.

He had told his client that he would be the lone spokesman. That Polly needed to keep silent. *Not a word. I'll handle it*, he had said repeatedly. And here she goes—two seconds in front of her husband and she's breaking down.

Carl Smith watched this. Saw the pleading look in Polly's eyes.

Noticed Iván's hand over his wife's. It was pale and hairless, with glossy manicured fingernails. And diamond-pinkie-ringed, of course.

When Escobar finally removed his hand, he reached down into the thin calfskin briefcase he had placed at his feet and removed a neatly folded single sheet of paper. He slid it toward Carl.

"This," he told Carl, "is a list of demands you will need to meet if you want to avoid an ugly and very public divorce proceeding."

Iván stayed eye to eye with Carl. Piece of cake.

Carl slid the paper the rest of the way, picked it up but didn't bother opening it. Instead, still locked in eye contact with Escobar, he tore it in two. Then slid the pieces back toward the divorce lawyer.

"Your services for my wife are no longer needed. You are discharged," he told Escobar. "Send me your bill for time spent. Put your thumb on the scale a little if you want. But send it. You will be promptly paid. Good-bye."

Iván smiled. Silently nodding his head. *That's the way you want to play it? Fine with me.*

Carl caught that. Momentarily jolted but quickly recovering, he broke eye contact and turned his attention instead to poor Polly.

"Dear," he said, "I'll take care of you, but not this way." Nodding in Escobar's direction. "Not with someone like him."

Another smile from Escobar. Another nod. He turned to his client.

"I think we're done here," he told her, rising. Then, to Carl, "Think it over. With me there are no second chances."

And then he escorted Polly from the room. He opened the door for her, and just as he guided her out, he turned once more toward Carl, still seated.

That look? If Carl didn't know better, he would have thought Iván's parting look was one of pity.

Iván quietly shut the door behind him.

Carl remained in his seat a beat or two longer than he normally might have.

The tropical sun was getting intense, rising directly above the palm trees at the edges of Carl's property. He checked his watch. Time to go in. He slid off his lounge and walked over to where William was seated on his bench doing dumbbell biceps curls.

He watched as William did another rep of ten, bulking his arm muscles even further. He liked seeing those protruding veins. Then William dropped the weights. He smiled up at Carl, gently put his hands on Carl's swim trunks, and slowly lowered them. Carl's erection popped into his face.

"Oh, my," William said.

Neither Carl nor William saw or heard anything, consumed in passion as they were. But they couldn't have anyway. It was too far off.

The private investigator hired by Iván Escobar was getting all this through the long telephoto lens as he rapidly clicked off one shot after another. The chartered boat was far enough offshore that its presence was unlikely to make itself known to Carl or William. It was just another boat out there in the ocean.

When the PI was satisfied that he had more than enough, he uploaded the digital photos to his laptop and e-mailed them to Escobar.

Within seconds Iván's laptop pinged with the new e-mail. He opened the attachment. Looked at the pictures. Sat back in his desk chair.

And smiled.

16.

There were three of us.

The two juniors I had been assigned and me. We had passed through security at the federal courthouse on Pearl Street in lower Manhattan and were standing in an upper-floor hallway waiting for the bailiff to unlock the doors to the courtroom.

This was to be our first appearance before the judge assigned to the GRE matter. It was just a status conference set by the court for scheduling, I had thought, nothing more. I didn't realize it at the time, but it was Peter Moss who had requested the conference. I think he should have given me the professional courtesy of letting me know in advance that was what he wanted. But he didn't. I was about to learn why.

It was mid-February, and winter had been in a rage the whole week. Sleet, snow, near-constant damp and freezing weather was propelled by wind gusts forcing all this at us from both rivers (East and Hudson). Wind ricocheted off buildings throughout the city, boomeranging icy bursts up and down its skyscraper-infested streets. We three were still in our coats, warming up in this underheated hallway.

I had finally caught up with my two juniors after Richard Miller's assault on my office. They got themselves up to speed quickly. By the time we walked into the courthouse, they knew as much about the case as I did.

"Here they come," Jeremy Lichtman said.

Two guys in suits and topcoats had just stepped out of the elevator bank at the far end of the hall and were coming our way. The middle-aged guy had to be Peter Moss, the younger one his junior.

Jeremy Lichtman was my fourth-year associate. I had worked with him on another case, but before I became a partner. I'd been the senior associate, and Jeremy had been one of a group of first- and second-years stuck with the vast bulk of the grunt work.

He was in some ways a strange guy, though average-looking, with horn-rimmed glasses and frizzy side-parted hair with an early bald spot. He was another Yalie, but you wouldn't know it from him. He didn't wear it pinned to his chest like some did. And there was a definite abrasive side to him, but he also could be wickedly funny in a Woody Allen sort of way. Plus, as I was soon to appreciate, he had a heart of gold.

The earlier case we had worked on was a suit between a CEO and his former New York Stock Exchange–listed company. The CEO had been lured away by a competitor and had left with his head (and laptop) filled with protected trade secrets. We represented the CEO's former company.

I don't know where the Dunn & Sullivan partner in charge had *his* head, but it certainly wasn't in the case. On the day before an important court hearing, he finally woke from his Rip van Winkle nap and realized that he needed to know the details of the lawsuit. Really know it, since in twenty-four hours he would be at counsel's table in court explaining to the judge why the defendant CEO shouldn't receive summary judgment against our client company.

Jeremy had been assigned the job of briefing the partner on all the legal issues he needed to master. The entire trial team was huddled around a table in one of the conference center's rooms. (Not that it matters, but it was the same room that Carl Smith later used for his meeting with Polly and Iván the Impaler.) Jeremy was brilliant, his mind an interstellar rocket. The problem was that the now-terrified partner's mind traveled at go-cart speed.

No one in that room will forget that meeting. It wasn't the only thing that sealed Jeremy's fate, so far as an eventual Dunn & Sullivan partnership was concerned, but it was right up there in a series of episodes that would torpedo his chances. Jeremy didn't care, as I later learned. He really didn't give a shit. He'd stay at the firm as long as they let him, and then he'd move on to something else.

So that meeting . . .

Like I said, Jeremy was briefing the partner, rattling off at break-neck speed the litany of legal issues the guy needed to know, explaining the pros, the cons, the relevant case law, and so on. The partner was panicking, trying to take notes, but Jeremy was going too fast for him. Keep in mind the guy hadn't done any of his homework.

". . . and so . . ." Jeremy was saying, head-down in his own notes. "There are three cases you need to ace on this point alone, because the judge will ask . . ."

The partner was drowning in information, and instead of throwing him a life preserver, Jeremy was dumping buckets of water over his head.

"Hold it, hold it, hold it," the partner said in near hysteria. "What are you saying? Is that the whatchacallit doctrine or the . . . the . . . ?"

(The *whatchacallit doctrine*? This guy was charging over a thousand dollars an hour for his time. Unbe-fucking-lievable.)

Here Jeremy, I think probably for the third time, rattled off the name of the legal doctrine, yet again explained its meaning. Why it mattered. Why there was a competing doctrine, its name, and why it mattered.

"Hold it. Hold it."

The partner again. He dropped his pen and raised his hands high over his head in the same gesture of surrender that the Germans did when captured at war's end.

Jeremy stopped. He waited, said nothing. Though his look across the table at the partner was unmistakable. *What a fucking dummy*, it said.

"Slower, slower," the partner pleaded, now pushing his open palms at Jeremy like he was carefully guiding the driver of a ten-wheeler trying to back his jumbo rig up to the warehouse loading dock.

Jeremy waited a good long minute. And then, dropping his voice several octaves, like a slow-motion recording, he said:

"Youuuu . . . represeeent . . . theeee . . . plainnnntiff. . . . Arrre . . . youuuu . . . withhh . . . meee . . . soooo . . . farrrr?"

Most of us around the table were busy biting our inner checks hard enough to stifle giggling. It was a bad career move to laugh at a partner. Especially one in the state this one was in.

Anyway, back to the courthouse hallway.

The approaching lawyer who was no doubt Peter Moss had pegged us for the opposition and so was heading our way, his junior in tow. He was smiling. The junior not so much.

"You take the older one," Jeremy said under his breath, "I'll take Tonto." Then adding, "Or we can let Gloria put them both down."

Gloria was Gloria Delarosa, our third team member, who was shaking her head at Jeremy. They had also worked together before and had become friends. Gloria was a paralegal. It was her second career. After the marines.

Gloria had been one of the few (experimental) women marines who'd seen actual combat. In both Iraq and Afghanistan. (My brother knew of her.) She had been awarded a Purple Heart, though I never did learn under what circumstances or how badly she'd been hit.

After mustering out of the Corps, she earned her paralegal certificate from Bronx Community College. Gloria was from a large Hispanic family, originally from Puerto Rico, I think, that had settled years ago in the upper reaches of eastern Manhattan, above Ninety-sixth Street, still known as Spanish Harlem.

Her dream was to become a lawyer. So far she had been rejected from every law school she'd applied to.

I don't know how to describe Gloria without saying she was virile—not masculine, really, but decidedly not feminine. She was stocky, wore her bleached hair female cut but military short. She had beautiful dark chocolate eyes, wore zero makeup, sported Angelina Jolie lips and a killer smile. Butch? That doesn't quite do it. I knew nothing about her private life. Even out of uniform, Gloria was still a marine. You could just see it.

"You must be Carney Blake."

I took Peter Moss's offered hand.

"Peter," Peter Moss said, meaning, *We'll be on first names here.* I must say I was somewhat surprised by this guy's warm and friendly behavior. This was a big case. We were adversaries. This was New York.

Introductions were made, handshakes all around. Peter's associate was a tall Asian guy named Harold Kim. He never said a word or cracked a smile.

"Bitter out there," Moss said, rubbing his hands together. Both he and Harold had also kept on their topcoats.

"Yeah," I said, not sure where this was going.

"Courtroom still locked?" Again with that beaming smile.

"Yeah. Bailiff should be around soon."

Looking at his watch. "He'd better."

More smiles.

"Uh-huh," was all I said.

"You been before this judge?" Moss asked.

"No. You?"

"A couple times. Smart. But a real stickler. Know what I mean?"

Just then the bailiff unlocked the courtroom doors from the inside. He ignored us standing out there in the hallway.

I didn't get a chance to answer Moss (now Peter to me, I guess).

He motioned for us to go in ahead of them, and we did, Moss still brandishing that gracious smile. I remember thinking that he must be one of those consummate professionals, the kind who never takes a client's position personally, always keeps his head above the fray.

Guess what?

17.

"r. Moss?"

Peter Moss stood facing the judge. Like I said ear-lier, he was a tall guy, about as tall as me, but he was thinner, more athletically built. He brushed away some loose strands of hair from his high forehead.

"You asked for this meeting," the judge continued.

"Yes, Your Honor, I did," Moss said.

I was sitting across the aisle at our table, Jeremy beside me and Gloria out in the gallery. (She was the only one out there.) I got an elbow nudge from Jeremy. When I looked at him, he mouthed, *What the fuck?*

Then, still on his feet, Moss turned and looked at me. No, that's not what happened. Still on his feet, Moss turned and *glared* at me.

Long enough for the judge to see.

"Okay," the judge said to him, impatient. "Tell us why we're here."

Judge Belinda Brown had been a federal judge for enough years to acquire that regal demeanor they all get sooner or later. And it's often accompanied with a large serving of judicial impatience.

The president, with the approval of the Senate, appoints federal judges. They serve for life. Minority judges don't exactly overpopu-late the federal judiciary. Our first black president had appointed her, and a substantial number of other African-American and Hispanic judges, many of them women.

Judge Brown looked like a judge. She was in her mid-forties, dark-skinned, with stern, unattractive features, eyeglasses even your grandmother wouldn't wear, and a hairdo like a helmet. She had on a necklace of white pearls pulled out over her judicial robe. Before her appointment she'd been a career federal prosecutor in the economic-crimes section of the Manhattan U.S. Attorney's office. Another mostly white bastion.

"Your Honor," Moss said, "as the court knows, we have filed a motion to dismiss this case. The other side has filed its opposition, and we have filed our reply to their opposition—"

"Yes, yes," Judge Brown said, interrupting. "You are telling me what I already know. What you are *not* telling me is why we're here."

"Yes, Your Honor," Moss said, waiting to see if there was more.

She looked at him and hunched her shoulders, letting him know. *What? What do you want?*

"Your Honor," Moss began, "this lawsuit is a fraud. It's a fraud on our client. And it's a fraud on this court. And we now believe that Mr. Blake's law firm is involved in this fraud."

Okay, I'll admit that last bit got the judge's attention.

I got another elbow from Jeremy. *Get up*, he was signaling. *Get to your feet. Object to this.*

I started to rise.

"Hold on, Mr. Blake," the judge said. "Let's hear Mr. Moss out, shall we?"

It wasn't a request.

I sat back down. I could feel Jeremy's heat.

"Thank you, Your Honor," Moss said, again glaring at me as though I had just confessed to strangling my mother.

"Your Honor," Moss said, "we have known for a while that the underlying case in which a judgment was given in an Indian court was procured by fraud. If we go back in time to—"

Impatience from the judge again.

"Get to the point, Counsel."

"Yes, Your Honor," Moss said, but I could tell he was going to milk this. The judge didn't intimidate him. I took note of that. It was the mark of experienced counsel. Someone who'd been in the ring enough times to know not to let a judge run his or her side of the case.

This might have been a good time for me to get back up and object. I didn't.

So Peter Moss rambled on. He told the judge that the Indian lawyer who had handled the case (not referring to him by name) had done some awful things. Craven and contemptible acts, without which there wouldn't have been a judgment rendered against his client in the first place.

And then.

"Your Honor, we have reason to believe that Mr. Blake's law firm discovered this fraud and decided to take on this case despite that. And that makes them complicit in what has become a continuing conspiracy."

A swift under-the-table kick from Jeremy put me back on my feet.

No sooner was I up than the judge waved me back down.

"You'll get your turn, Counsel," she said, not unkindly, I (wrongly) thought.

"Yes, Your Honor," I said, re-taking my seat.

Was I being too passive? What would Peter Moss be doing if the tables were turned? Moss's "reason to believe" was just another "on information and belief" ploy. Wasn't it? Just more bullshit word twisting? Shouldn't I have been up, vocal, objecting, even if the judge tried gaveling me down?

Jeremy Lichtman's under-his-breath "Give me a fucking break" didn't help things.

I watched as poker-faced Harold Kim handed Moss a batch of papers.

"Your Honor," Moss said, holding the papers aloft like some severed head.

Jeremy kicked me again. I stood.

"Cool your motors, Counsel," she warned me. "You'll get your chance."

"Thank you, Your Honor."

That wasn't me. That was Moss.

He walked over to where I was once again seated and handed me the pack of papers. Our eyes met. His back was to the judge. That benevolent smile was once more on his face. He even winked at me.

In the words of Jeremy Lichtman: Give me a fucking break.

When Moss turned to face the court, he was again all seriousness and righteous indignation.

"Your Honor," he said, "I have given opposing counsel a copy of a new complaint. We have not yet filed it with the clerk of court. In it we name Dunn & Sullivan as the defendant. We believe they knowingly took on and are pursuing a case built on fraud and corruption."

Again I rose. Again the judge impatiently waved me back down.

"Shouldn't your complaint be a counterclaim filed in this case against Mr. Blake's law firm?" the judge asked, involuntarily shooting a glance my way. (What? She's now co-counsel with Moss, discussing litigation strategy?)

"No, Your Honor, our motion to dismiss is pending. When we get to argue it, we are confident you will grant the motion and throw that case out of court. But whether you do or you don't, our client wants this separate, stand-alone case against Dunn & Sullivan for fraud."

"So you're filing this new complaint?"

"Maybe."

That was a bad answer. Even experienced counsel can make mistakes.

"Maybe?" the judge said, with what sounded to me like the beginning of something more than impatience.

"It depends," Moss said.

"On what?"

"On whether Dunn & Sullivan withdraw their asset-seizure case and acknowledge that they should never have taken it on in the first place."

Let's hit the PAUSE button here for a minute.

Look, no way did Peter Moss expect me to dismiss my case. No fucking way. So what was he up to? At the time I really didn't know. Hadn't figured it out yet. Of course, later I would.

This was a setup. Moss had every intention of suing Dunn & Sullivan. Had from the beginning. He was just dragging things out to make us look bad. No, worse. Corrupt. And our Dipak Singh? His name was not going to cross Peter Moss's lips.

He wasn't going to name Singh or sue him. That was part of the deal, don't you see?

Like I said earlier, Dipak had selected Dunn & Sullivan to be his clients' American counsel. His co-counsel. But it was Peter Moss, Dipak's opposing counsel, who'd been behind our selection. Dipak chose us only after Peter Moss had *paid him* to do it. But Dipak must have gotten something else besides his under-the-table money. And what would that be?

An assurance. A promise. Peter Moss must have promised Dipak that no matter what Peter did to us in the case, he would not do anything to Dipak. Dipak would not be sued as we were about to be. Dipak was free and clear.

For him this was a win-win situation.

If ultimately the GRE case were lost, there would be no contingent legal fee for him, or for Dunn & Sullivan. But Dipak gets to keep his *Peter Moss* payment. If the case is won, why, then Dipak still gets to keep his Moss money *and* he makes a shitload of money on his contingent fee.

Would we bring Dipak into the case? Technically we could. We'd claim that we didn't do anything wrong, but if anything wrong in fact occurred, it was on him and not us. But as a practical matter, if Dipak did anything wrong, why were we still in the case, trying our best to win it? No, Dipak got himself a pass.

Would it last? Good question.

Okay, roll the tape.

The judge looked long and hard at Moss. "Counsel," she finally said, "you *believe* that Mr. Blake's law firm involved itself in this fraud?" (See?) "On what do you base this *belief*?"

"Your Honor, with respect, I can't disclose our evidence, coming as it does from confidential sources."

(Yeah, right.)

The judge finally turned to me, but she was already steaming.

"Okay, Mr. Blake. Your turn."

As I rose to speak, my mind racing, grasping for the right words, I realized I couldn't take the same tack as Moss. Couldn't say, *Well, Your Honor, as far as I* know *or to the best of my* belief *Dunn & Sullivan was not involved in any fraud here.* This judge would think I was waffling. And if she saw me waffling, she was going to start wondering if there was some fire behind all the smoke that Peter Moss was blowing.

So I didn't think about right or wrong. This wasn't the time to reexamine if Dunn & Sullivan was blameless, as I really thought we were. After all, this case came to me directly from Carl Smith. The chairman of the goddamn law firm.

Maybe it wasn't the time. But time is what I took too much of. It was Judge Brown who was now on fire, waiting for me to say something. I cleared my throat. Waited another beat to make sure I would have a voice when I opened my mouth.

"Your Honor," I began, "this is outrageous—"

And that's as far as I got before the judge exploded. (I really should have forced myself into this debate before now.)

Turning to Moss. "Counsel," she said, motioning him back to his feet. So that both of us were standing before her.

"Now, listen, you two," she said, wagging a finger at each of us in turn. "Someone is playing games with this court. And I don't like it. Not one bit. So here's what we are going to do. We are going to have some extensive discovery in this case. Written interrogatories. Depositions. Full disclosure. Each of you will disclose to the other what you've got. We are going to get to the bottom of this. And when we do, each of you better pray that your hands are clean. Are we clear on that?"

Me and Moss (a chorus of two): "Yes, Your Honor."

"That's it, then," the judge said, nodding down to her bailiff, who quickly stood.

"All rise!" he shouted to the mostly empty courtroom.

And after the judge and bailiff disappeared through a side door, Peter Moss came over to me, again all smiles. He shook my hand.

"Told you she was a stickler," he said, like we were pals, in this together.

I shook his hand. Said nothing. Uncertain really what to say. There was enough heat coming off Jeremy, standing behind me, to fry a chicken.

"Look, let's get together," Moss told me. "Lunch maybe, and work out a discovery schedule. Something we can both live with."

Lunch?

If Moss saw how flabbergasted I was, he certainly hid it well.

"So," he continued, all hunky-dory, "I'll give you a call."

Another big smile. Then, with a little wave of his hand—*Bye, see you soon*—Moss returned to his table to collect his papers.

Harold Kim was looking our way. Smirking.

I got a little push in my back from Jeremy. I turned.

"We need to talk," he said. Not happy.

Not happy at all.

And he was right. In my defense, it's one thing to be at table assisting and another to be the one standing on your feet and speaking. But he was right. I hadn't handled that well. I needed first-chair experience. You didn't get that very quickly in big law firms, not as a freshly minted partner. You assisted more senior partners who tutored you along the way. Until it was your time and you were ready. That was how it was supposed to work.

Not like this, learning as you go, on your own, and on the client's nickel.

Okay, fine, but for better or worse I was first chair here.

I had to be smarter. And do better.

18.

I was having lunch with Carl Smith.

That is, I was supposed to be having lunch with Carl Smith. I got to the restaurant ten minutes early, and twenty minutes later still no Carl.

And the fact that I needed to pee, really needed to pee, wasn't helping. (I didn't want to be in the bathroom when—and by that time, I was thinking, if—Carl Smith walked in.) So how did this luncheon come about?

After last week's hearing, Jeremy, Gloria, and I left the courthouse rebundled against the cold and walked up Pearl Street to Centre and then turned on Worth for the Starbucks there. It was bitter out; it hurt your face just to walk those few blocks.

By then it was about 11:30 a.m. The Starbucks was steamy warm and mostly empty. We ordered our coffees and sat at one of the tables in the back, piling our coats, hats, scarves, gloves on the empty fourth chair.

Once we'd settled in, I made no bones about the fact that I had fucked up. A blind man could have seen that I was down on myself.

"Well," Jeremy said, prying the lid off his overheated no-foam skim latte and blowing on it.

"Well what?" I said.

Jeremy looked at me for a while. Thinking, then he smiled. "Fuck Peter Moss. Fuck Judge What's-her-name. We're better than them."

"Really?"

"Well . . . ?"

Gallows humor. We chuckled. It relieved some tension.

Gloria hadn't said a word. Not being a lawyer put her more in the ranks of an enlisted person than an officer. By instinct and military training, she wasn't about to volunteer anything but would speak her mind when asked.

"And you?" I asked.

I watched as Gloria took a sip of her espresso macchiato. She grimaced, then looked around for the serving table where the milk and sugar were kept, then apparently thought better of it. Took a second sip, seemed to decide it'd do as is. I could see the cord of muscle in her neck.

"What do I think? We got our asses kicked, that's what I think," she said, shrugging. "So what?" she continued, pursing those Jolie lips. "The case is just starting. You know, like they say, fuck me once, shame on you. Fuck me twice . . ."

Jeremy and I chimed in, "Shame on me."

"Okay, so how do we prevent a repeat performance?" I asked.

And as I did, I braced myself for Jeremy telling me what I was afraid to hear: that this case needed a full-time, experienced litigation partner. Someone senior to me. Someone for *me* to assist. There would be no punches pulled by him. None.

"What you need," he said, "what this case needs . . ." He bent to sip at his coffee, leaving the cup on the table. "What it needs is a rabbi."

"A what?"

"A rabbi. A godfather. Someone at the firm you can consult with from time to time. A seasoned sideline coach."

Back to my still-no-show Carl Smith luncheon.

The waiter came by for the umpteenth time and topped up my water glass. I had ordered a Diet Coke when I got here. Drank that, and since then I'd been sipping at this bottomless glass of ice water. My bladder was about to burst.

After Jeremy, Gloria, and I left Starbucks and got back to Dunn & Sullivan's Times Square offices, I shot off an e-mail to Smith. It was short. I felt I needed to report to him. This was a case he'd brought in. He was the responsible partner. And I wanted to ask him for a rabbi, as Jeremy (to my relief) had suggested.

I kept a print copy of the e-mail:

To: Carl Smith
From: Carney Blake
Subject: GRE

Carl:
We were in court today on the GRE matter. It did not go well. I would like to brief you.

Carney Blake
Partner
Dunn & Sullivan, LLP
One Times Square
New York, NY 10036

That's all I wrote. It wasn't until later that I learned putting anything in writing was a problem. For Smith.

Two days after my e-mail, his secretary called and told me that I was to meet him for lunch that day, 12:30 p.m. sharp, at DB Bistro Moderne on West Forty-Fourth Street.

"Be on time," she admonished me. "Mr. Smith has a full schedule."

When I got to the restaurant, I was told that indeed Mr. Smith's office had booked a table in his name, and once I relinquished my topcoat, I was shown to that table. Right behind me was a tropical-fish tank. The bubbling sound from the tank's water-filtration system was not helping my need to pee.

And so there I sat. I was about to get up and chance a quick men's-room run when I saw Carl Smith being led to our table by the hostess. I stood to shake hands. Smith didn't even look at me before taking the seat opposite. I sat back down.

In the blink of an eye, our waiter was tableside.

"Good afternoon, Mr. Smith," he said, with a deference befitting a head of state.

In New York so many young waiters and waitresses are out-of-work or looking-for-work actors. And they bring their personas to their daytime jobs. Like this guy. Beautifully styled wavy brown hair, wonderful teeth, just effeminate enough to wonder.

Smith didn't respond.

"Shall I tell you the specials?" the waiter said, flashing a game-show-host smile. A performance in the wings here.

"No," Smith said. Then, ignoring the waiter (servers were apparently not deserving of the Carl Smith preprogrammed charm offensive) and addressing me instead. "Know what you want?"

While waiting, I had studied the portfolio-size menu I'd been handed when seated.

"Yeah," I told Smith.

Back to the waiter, with Smith's unopened menu resting on his starched white napkin.

"Lobster salad. Iced tea," he just about snarled.

Even though he was perhaps a wannabe actor, this was New York. And DB Bistro Moderne was no ordinary restaurant in this town. So this waiter had been schooled in how to read the clientele. In a flash the smile disappeared.

"Very good," the waiter said, with the seriousness of an undertaker solacing the bereaved. Then, lifting his head my way, an unspoken, *And you?*

"The burger," I said, then quickly added, "Medium," before the waiter could ask what kind of coffin I would like that in.

"And to drink?" The waiter stood poised, note pad and pen at the ready.

To drink? My bladder was ballooning. One more sip of anything and Diet Coke–flavored ice water would start leaking from my ears and nose.

Pointing at my half-empty water glass. "I'm good with this."

The waiter disappeared and in a flash returned with a frosted metal pitcher and refilled my glass. Just what I needed.

The fish tank's circulating water kept gurgling.

With the waiter finally gone, Carl . . . well, waited.

(If I didn't go soon . . .)

"Things didn't go well in court . . ." I began.

Carl said nothing, listening to my tale of woe until I got to Moss.

"Peter Moss?" he asked. Carl had paid so little attention to the case that he didn't even know who was on the other side.

"You know him?"

The strangest of smiles crossed Carl's face. Really weird. Couldn't read it. "Classmates at Harvard. He was an associate here."

Meaning at Dunn & Sullivan. So Peter Moss had been an associate at our law firm? And then not? That probably meant let go, I was thinking. Passed over for partnership. But I remember also thinking that there seemed more to it, given the look on Smith's face. Of course, I didn't know then what I know now.

So I went on.

When I got to the part about the judge ordering full discovery, he again stopped me.

"How long?" he asked.

"How long what?"

By this time I was really having trouble concentrating. The fish tank's gurgling in my ears seemed so much louder now.

"You all right?"

"What?"

"Are you all right?"

"Fine." (*Never better, though I'm about to piss my pants.*) I shifted in my seat.

Act natural. Look normal, I told myself.

Like Carl. Who looked just fine. Like always.

I noticed his tan. Must have been away someplace warm, I remember thinking. He was in one of his tailored-to-perfection suits. This one so deep blue it was almost purple, his shirt and tie in perfectly matching lighter shades of complementing hues. An ensemble. Even Carl's hair was fluffed just right. Did he have a stylist come to his apartment each morning with a hairbrush?

What was he asking?

"The discovery?" Carl prodded.

The discovery. The discovery what? Oh. How long?

"A year," I told him.

That seemed to please him. (He wanted the delay of anything happening in the case until after the IPO, of course.)

A different server approached with Carl's lobster salad and another with his iced tea. The restaurant had a system, I guessed, for how to get orders to diners. Then our waiter was back.

He ran his eyes over the table.

"Everything okay, Mr. Smith?" he said.

A nod was all he got from Carl. Then the waiter told me there was a slight backup in the kitchen and that my burger would be out any minute now.

Carl began eating. He seemed in a hurry. Months later, when Carl's electronic calendar was put into evidence, it showed that he had a 2:15 p.m. meeting that day with the investment bankers. The schedule bore the notation "finishing touches."

"Blake," Carl said between mouthfuls. (What happened to "Carney"?) "Do not send me any more e-mails or any memos. Is that clear?"

I nodded.

"You want me? You pick up the phone and call me."

He waited for my acknowledgment.

"Understood."

"Nothing in writing," he admonished, pointing his fork at me like he was about to stab me with it.

Okay, okay, I got it but wondered all the same what was the big deal here? Not yet realizing that Carl wanted deniability should anything go wrong in the case. There was to be no record of our communications.

Carl went back to gobbling his lunch. I had the feeling that he was now done with me. I was peripheral. He had said what he needed to say.

It's now or never, my bladder signaled.

"Be right back," I said as I got up from the table. Carl didn't look up from his plate as I race-walked to the men's room.

When I got there, I tried the door handle. Locked.

I waited as long as I could, then I jiggled the handle.

"Out in a minute," the guy inside said.

After another full minute, another jiggle.

"Hold your horses," the guy inside said, with clear and understandable annoyance.

But I needed to go. Standing here so close and yet so far made matters even worse. I tried the ladies'. The door opened. Unoccupied.

I went in. Raised the toilet seat, unzipped, and waited. I was so backed up that nothing wanted to come out. I felt the pressure, but nothing.

"Jesus fucking Christ," I said, probably too loud, but hey, I was alone in there and I was bursting.

And then it came. A small stream, a bigger stream, and there it was. Relief.

"Ahhhhhhh," I moaned out loud. "Ahhhhhh."

When I finished, I quickly washed my hands and opened the door. The woman who had been standing there waiting to use the ladies' gave me such a look. *I heard you in there*, it said. *You pervert. Masturbating, middle of the day. And in the ladies'.*

I tried a sheepish smile. She glared at me and shook her head. *You are filth.*

And what do I do? Flustered, I quickly shut the door. Then, after a beat, I opened it again. Like where was I going to go? When I opened it, she was gone. Once back at our table, I saw her seated at hers, whispering to the three other women lunching with her. Two of them were giving me the evil eye.

When I made it back to our table, no Carl Smith. His lobster salad had been cleared away. Ditto his iced tea. He could have gone to the men's room and found it unoccupied while I was moaning and groaning in the ladies'. Somehow I didn't think so. On the table was the folder for the check. When I sat down, I opened it. Smith had paid the bill. I saw our waiter approach with my burger.

He placed it before me.

"I brought this out when you were in the bathroom. Mr. Smith told me to hold it until you got back."

"Thanks," I said, looking around the restaurant. No sign of Smith.

Reading my mind. "Mr. Smith is no longer with us." (This guy was taking the undertaker role too seriously.)

"Gone?" I said.

Gone, he confirmed with a funereal nod of his head.

19.

She was Jeremy Lichtman's idea.

I suppose I could have called Carl Smith and asked him for the rabbi I never had the chance to bring up over lunch. But Smith had made himself pretty clear: *Leave me out of it*. He never said it that way, but a rocket-science degree wasn't necessary to read him. And, yes, I thought back on that many times.

I met with Jeremy and Gloria in my office the day after the lunch. I told them what had happened. (Without the ladies'-room part.)

They seemed to take what I said at face value. Looking back on it, should they—or should I, for that matter—have been suspicious about Carl's luncheon behavior? Yeah, sure, with hindsight I can say that. But we weren't. Okay, maybe shame on us. But the truth of the matter is, we weren't.

"So," Jeremy said. "Do what you need to do."

"Meaning?"

"Get your own rabbi."

He was right. I looked at Gloria. She conveyed nothing. This was above her pay grade. Fair enough.

Okay, let's see, I was thinking, who in the litigation department could I go to? What experienced partner would give up otherwise billable hours to confer off the record with me? Meaning said litigation partner would receive zero compensation from said law firm for helping me. The chances of that happening at Dunn & Sullivan? Slim to none, I decided.

"I've got just the person," Jeremy said.

Not two hours later, there I was in her office.

Anka Stankowski was known in the firm's hallways as "Jabba the Hutt." She weighed in somewhere seriously north of two-fifty. As, by the way, did her husband, a partner in another big law firm in the city. They were his-and-her sumo wrestlers in lawyer's clothing. I remembered seeing them dancing together at last year's Christmas gala. They were surprisingly light on their toes, even though they looked like a couple of hippos in an animated Disney film.

Anka was powering down. She was less than a year away from the firm's mandatory retirement age (sixty-eight). She was as smart and experienced a litigator as the firm had to offer. Jeremy's thinking was that Anka could well afford to help me. She had made a pile of money at the firm. As had her husband at his. She was on her way out. She really had nothing to lose and might be willing to meet with me from time to time.

"Come on in," Anka said as I stood in her open doorway. "Have a seat."

Anka was behind her desk, looking like a container ship docked at its berth, but friendly, smiling at me, motioning me to a chair. Her belly protruded, her head was covered with a thick carpet of white hair. She had coal-gray eyes and ham-hock arms. When I got myself seated and was closer, I noticed the peach fuzz covering her cheeks and a simple gold wedding ring embedded in her sausage finger.

"Thanks for seeing me," I said.

"What's up?"

"Well, I need some help," I said, and then launched into the summary of where we were in the case and what I wanted from her. I was midway through my story when I heard a hard thump on the frame of Anka's open door. I instinctively turned. There stood Richard Miller, glaring. He had tracked me down.

I'd done nothing on his cases. Absolutely nothing.

Pointing his finger at me like an executioner pointing to the one next in line for the gallows.

"You," he said, reversing his hand and beckoning me with his index finger.

I turned and looked at Anka.

As I said earlier, word was out on Miller.

"Not now," she dismissively told Miller.

"Yes now."

"Richard, get the fuck out of here. He's meeting with me. He'll see you later."

"Not good enough," Richard said.

I was ping-ponging between them. While looking at Miller, I heard this stage sigh from Anka.

"Richard," Anka said with bored annoyance, leaning forward in her chair, laying those enormous arms on her desk. "How fucking hard is this for you to understand? He's meeting with me. Go away."

Like I said, Anka was a heavyweight at Dunn & Sullivan. (Figuratively speaking at the moment.) So was Miller, but he could not best her if it came to it. He knew that.

And sure enough he stormed off. All well and good, but guess who was going to pay the price for this mini–Mexican standoff?

"You're working for him?" Anka said, like, *Didn't you get the memo?*

I told her what had happened when Miller barged into my office.

"Okay," Anka said. "Leave it with me."

I looked at her, pantomiming, *Leave it with me what?*

100

"Just leave it with me."

And so I went back to the GRE story.

I must say that Anka listened intently, even to the point of making periodic notes on the legal pad in front of her.

"Interesting," she said when I finally finished. "I didn't know we were now taking plaintiffs' class-action cases. We've always been on the defense side."

And she made a note of that.

I guess we do now, I shrugged.

"Interesting," she repeated. "And Carl was the case initiator?"

"Uh-huh."

"Who's paying our fee?"

That was above *my* pay grade, so it got a dunno shrug.

Another note on Anka's legal pad.

"What's this Indian lawyer like?" she asked.

As I started explaining that I'd talked to the guy on the phone but hadn't met him, Anka was shaking her head no, no, no.

She ripped the top sheet off her legal pad and then tossed the pad over to me. "Got a pen?"

I grabbed a ballpoint from the inside pocket of my suit jacket.

I then got Anka's tutorial. A lot of what she said I think I could have eventually pulled together on my own. Not all, but a lot. Except I hadn't, and it was helpful to hear from her the list of things I needed to do to protect the case.

Among what she told me:

1. Get Dipak Singh's ass to New York PDQ and keep him here until he has been thoroughly (*And I mean thoroughly*, Anka said, and I duly noted) debriefed.
2. Don't wait for Peter Moss and his discovery demands. Figure out what you'd be asking for if you were Moss and collect and analyze that shit ("shit" was Anka's word) now.

3. You need to find any holes in your case before the other side does.

4. If you find any holes in your case, start plugging them now.

5. Use Jeremy Lichtman's outsize brain as much as possible. (Anka seemed well aware of Jeremy's peculiarities but clearly felt they were trumped by his abilities.)

There were about twenty or twenty-five other line items she had me write down, but you get the picture. When she finished, she sat back in her chair. There went that belly, floating up like an emerging landmass at low tide.

"Door's open anytime," she told me.

Walking back to my office, I felt better. I had my sideline coach. And I thought back on that many times, too.

20.

Was Dipak Singh ignoring me?

I had placed three calls to him in India over the last several days. I left clear, detailed recorded messages. I never heard back. That didn't necessarily mean he was avoiding me. Maybe it was the time zone (though I called during *his* business hours). Or he could have been in court. Could have been away. Could have been anything. I should have e-mailed him. So I was in my office doing just that when my cell rang.

I looked at the screen. Was that Dipak finally calling me back? Nope, the call was from the Hell's Kitchen landline. That meant my old man. Sean and Rosy had cells. My father didn't. Who was he going to call? Except me, apparently. I tapped on the screen's green ACCEPT circle.

"Hi," I said, my gaze on the laptop screen as I proofed my e-mail before sending. There was silence on the other end of the line. "Dad?"

"Get over here."

"What?"

"I said get over here, boy."

I could hear something in his voice. Fear? No way, I thought. Not from the mighty Seamus Blake.

"Dad, I'm at the office."

"You. Here. Now."

And then he hung up. I speed-dialed my brother. Got voice mail. Next Rosy. Voice mail for her. Then I called the apartment landline. It just rang until I got voice mail there, too. One of those computer-generated messages, the mechanical male voice choppily telling me, *"You. Have. Dialed. 212 . . ."*

All right, something was up. I needed to go and see what the hell it was. I hit SEND on the Dipak e-mail, then grabbed my suit jacket and overcoat off the hook behind my door.

I cabbed it up to the apartment. Didn't take long. I have a key to the street-level door, so I let myself in and climbed the stairs. The apartment door was ajar, the living room empty.

"Dad?"

"In here," my father called from Rosy and Sean's bedroom.

I took off my topcoat and tossed it to the sofa. The bedroom door was open. Rosy was seated on the edge of the bed, eyes fluttering, shoulders slumped, head drooping. She had on jeans but no top, just a threadbare bra. My father stood facing her, stone-still, helpless.

"Your brother's on a rampage," he told me. "He's gone off for the fella that done this."

"Done what?"

"He took his .45."

I had to drag it out of him question by question as his head began swiveling between me and poor, strung-out Rosy. His face had drained of all color. Rosy's eyes kept fluttering, her head dipping.

What I pulled from him was that last week Rosy had indeed over-dosed. On heroin. Sean and he had rushed her to Mount Sinai West on Tenth Avenue. Even though Sean was deep into crystal meth, he had been infuriated with Rosy. Once home, in a teary shouting match with my brother, Rosy had promised to stay clear of her new dealer and no more smack.

When earlier that morning Sean had found Rosy seated on the toilet, semidressed like now, nodding off, a crumpled strip of aluminum foil, glassine bag, syringe, and Bic lighter on the sink ledge beside her, he lost it. After grabbing his .45 from his sock drawer, he stormed out of the apartment. He knew the dealer. Rosy had told him who the guy was last week in the emergency ward. Sean had gone and confronted the guy. Told him if he sold anything ever again to Rosy, Sean would come back and shoot him dead on the spot.

I knelt in front of Rosy, put my hands on her thighs, and gently squeezed. She opened her eyes, saw me.

"Hey, Carney," she said with that angelic Rosy smile. Then nodded off.

"Rosy," I said, squeezing her thighs again. "Where's Sean?"

Another smile. Another drop-off.

It took a little while, but I managed to get a name and address for her new dealer.

You know, I didn't see Rosy much. And never before like this. Sweet Rosy, so important to my brother. This kind and tender soul. Over the last few weeks, she had from time to time called me, always late at night. Slurring her words, telling me how happy she was that I, too, now had a girlfriend. Telling me, "Be nice to her, Carn, okay, baby?" And I'd say, "You bet, Rosy." "Love you, Carn," she'd always say as she clicked off. *Love you, too, Rosy*, I would think as I lowered my phone.

"Keep her awake," I told my father. "Walk her around if you can."

I grabbed my topcoat from the sofa and quickly left the apartment.

21.

I stepped from the cab at 112th Street.

On the way over here, I thought about calling Gloria Delarosa and asking for help. This was her old neighborhood. Then decided no. My private life was my private life. It had nothing to do with my career. Best to keep them separate.

What if I was too late? What if Sean had already killed this guy?

I stood before the shabby apartment building, passersby giving me the once-over. Me standing in this neighborhood looking all Brooks Brothers.

My thinking here was admittedly fluid. This situation was moving fast, probably too fast. My brother was in a murderous rage. I just had to find him and stop him from doing something that would either put him in prison for life or take his life. He, after all, was gunning for a drug dealer, not some pea-brained goose eyeing a collection of plastic decoys.

I really didn't have time to reason this out. Maybe later, I thought. Right now I just needed to find my brother. Hopefully before it was too late. Sean was coming undone—had been, of course, since

Afghanistan—and the crystal meth was accelerating his downward trajectory.

I raced up the worn steps, located the name on the faded tenant list, and pushed the button next to it.

A crackling voice came over the intercom. "What?"

So far so good. The guy up there was still alive.

"I'm looking for Sean Blake."

Nothing.

I was about to jam my finger back on the button when the door buzzer sounded. I quickly grabbed the handle and entered the vestibule. It was dark and damp, the wallpaper was peeling, and there was the unmistakable reek of stale piss and staler garbage.

The apartment was on the second floor. I took the steps fast as I could. Quickly located the apartment and knocked on the door. Again nothing. I pounded on it. The door opened.

I stood there in that fetid hallway. Across the threshold was a guy, clearly Latino, pointing a silver pistol at my face. We stood there like that for what seemed an eternity. Then the guy took a few backward steps and used his gun to wave me into the apartment.

Once inside, I could tell from a quick glance around. This piece-of-shit living room was just a distribution place. No one lived here. It was probably one of several such locations he had throughout the city.

The man pointing the gun at me looked about my age. He was thin, dark, in that nether region between Spanish and African. His face was pockmarked. He was wearing steel-rimmed John Lennon eyeglasses. There were two other guys in the room. Also Latino. Big guys seated side by side on a ratty sofa. They were both in dark suits and open-necked shirts. One guy's massive head was shaved, and he sported a stubble beard. The other had a ponytail. They kept watchful eyes on me.

The guy with the gun was checking me out, too. While that pistol looked to me the size of a small cannon, I did manage a quick glance at his eyes. I saw puzzlement. At least I think I did.

"And?" the guy finally said.

"I'm Sean Blake's brother."

"Good for you."

"Listen, I said. "You know this, but my brother's girlfriend buys—"

"Stop," the guy ordered. He cocked his gun.

I stopped.

He then nodded to the shaved-headed guy, who lifted himself off the couch and came over to where I was standing. He signaled for me to hold my arms out to my sides, and then he frisked me.

"Clean," he said to the boss.

"A wire," the boss told him, like, *Do I have to spell out every fucking little thing for you?* The guy nodded. *Oh, okay.*

"Take off your clothes," this hulking blockhead then told me.

"What?"

"Down to your skivvies. You do it or I do it for you. Up to you, man."

The three of them watched while I undressed. As I removed each item of clothing, he took it from me, patted it down for any electronics, and then neatly folded the item and lowered it to the chair near us. Neatly? Like what, he was my valet?

Then I was down to my skivvies. The big guy even had me take off my socks. He nodded to the guy with the gun.

"Clean," he said.

"His wallet."

The big guy removed my wallet from my trousers and tossed it over to him. He snatched it with his left hand, lowered the gun, and stuffed it into the waistband of his trousers. He then went through my wallet, removed my driver's license and one of my business cards. I watched as he went to a laptop sitting on a nearby table, where there was also a scale and collection of stuffed glassine bags.

He Googled me. I stood there watching as he went onto the Dunn & Sullivan website, clicked on the "Professionals" tab and then the "Partners" directory. He saw my picture, read my bio.

"What the fuck are you doing here?" he said. "You should be smarter than this, Counselor."

I shrugged.

When you're right, you're right.

22.

Diane's Long Island City apartment was so much nicer than mine.

I was a transient in my apartment. Diane lived in hers. It was a home. We liked to sleep there Saturday nights. That way we could enjoy slow Sunday mornings. Fresh coffee and bagels. The Sunday *Times*. And that Manhattan skyline. Not bad.

The weather was letting up. Finally. Sunlight flooded into the apartment, brightening everything. Diane had just handed me the front page of the paper. Her hair was still all frizzed from the night before. She tightened the cloth belt on her robe; it had the unintended effect of silhouetting her figure. That got my attention. I loved being around her. Our relationship was deepening, no doubt about it. And not just physically. When I think back on it, this is when I started really falling in love with her.

"Check it out," she said playfully, adding, "the paper," with an over-the-shoulder grin as I watched her sashay back to the kitchen counter and the coffeemaker.

As you can see, I made it out of Spanish Harlem alive.

After the dealer finished Googling me, he stayed seated at the

table and had the thug with the ponytail put me in the chair facing him.

"Can I get dressed?" I asked.

"Not just yet."

Taking away someone's clothes does intimidate. I never really
appreciated how much until I sat there in my underpants facing this
guy. Of course, the two big guys on the sofa and that pistol now on
the table next to the laptop didn't exactly put me at ease either.

He kept watching me, puzzled. I needed to say something. I
couldn't just sit there like that.

"Where are we going with this?" I finally asked.

"You tell me, Counselor."

"My brother's gunning for you."

That got a smirk from him and chuckles from the two behemoths
on the couch.

"I'm terrified," he said to more laughter. Adding, "So you want
what?"

I told him my brother's story.

The dealer shrugged. He couldn't have cared less.

"You coming here like this? A lawyer in some big fucking law
firm? You gotta admit this is pretty stupid."

I think I was seated in one of the only old and decrepit New York
apartments that didn't drench you in oppressive steam heat. I was
shivering. I'm sure he saw that.

What could I say? Okay, this wasn't the most thoughtful thing I'd
ever done. But time still seemed to be of the essence. With Sean out
there somewhere, waiting for this guy to show his head so he could
put a bullet in it.

"I want you to cut his girlfriend off," I told him. "No more dope.
And I'll get my brother to stand down."

One of the guys on the couch said something in Spanish. I only
caught a word or two, not enough to understand.

"Carlos thinks that instead of cutting your girl off, we should cut your balls off," the dealer told me, "and send them to your brother. Show him what will happen to his own cojones he comes 'round here again."

Wonderful. *What now?* I was thinking.

"But you do have balls, coming here," he added. "I'll give you that, Counselor. So now listen. . . ."

Diane put a fresh mug of coffee on the table beside me as I read the Sunday *Times* piece she had pointed out. Entitled "Big Law's Unhappy Weight Loss," it was the lead article running from the front page to three full inside pages. The *Times* does that, you know? Leads with a long article on Sunday, figuring you've got more leisure to read than during busy weekday mornings.

So what did it say?

It talked about law-firm defections, lawyers jumping ship because revenue was down. They were deserting and climbing aboard other big firms in search of ever-higher paydays. About clients complaining, demanding lower fees, objecting to associate leveraging, and a good number of those clients abandoning ship, too. It said that some of the older firms were losing both lawyers and clients at unprecedented levels, putting them in jeopardy of sinking for the first time in their long and distinguished histories.

Dunn & Sullivan was mentioned, though with not a word written about Carl Smith's scheme to take the firm public. That hadn't leaked yet. And nothing about Peter Moss. His law firm was still not in the ranks of Big Law. So nothing about him either.

I can't say that this was all news to me. You heard things. But only in a gossipy way. Corridor talk. Competition between the major law firms was fierce, so there was no sharing of stories among them, no comparison of woes.

What the *Times* did was put all the separate pieces together and then place them in the Sunday edition as a comprehensive story. This was the first public disclosure of what had apparently been brewing for some time. And the *Times* piece would no doubt generate follow-on stories from other publications. And the more stories, the more likely there would be hard shoves to the backs of more law firms standing blindfolded on the lip of the abyss.

When I finished reading, I lowered the paper and took hold of the mug at my elbow. I sipped at my coffee and sat there thinking. Here I had worked so hard, had put in an ungodly number of hours year in and year out so that I could make it, be a part of this world. A world in trouble. And how did I feel?

Good question.

I had felt more alive up in that ratty Spanish Harlem apartment than at any time since law school. Fair enough, but I still wanted to be part of this world, coming as I had from the outside, from the so-called working class. For all its woes, Big Law was still something substantial. It would redefine me. Make me something different, something better.

What did this say about me?

I looked over at Diane in the kitchen area, her back to me as she waited for a bagel in the toaster. Did she agonize over her professional life like this? A government lawyer exchanging hard work for soft pay? Remember, she couldn't even afford this apartment after the next rent hike. Still, she seemed a great deal happier with her lot than I did with mine. But did she secretly aspire to something more? Like I said, I didn't ask. Should I have?

Of course I should have.

And then I shut it down. I mean, what was the point? I was committed. What was I going to do? Throw up my hands and just leave? No way. I had a case. A meaningful one with injured clients. No way was I about to abandon them.

I reached over to the coffee table for the sports pages.

. . .

When the drug dealer finally let me put my clothes back on, I got out of that apartment as fast as I could. No sooner had I set foot on the sidewalk than my cell chimed. It was Sean.

"What the fuck you doin'?" he said.

"Where are you?"

"Across the street, to your right."

I searched up the block. There was Sean, behind a parked car on the far side of the street. Waiting for the dealer. His hoodie up over his head for cover. The .45 no doubt jammed in his pocket. I walked across to him, grabbed his elbow, and forced him away.

I made a deal up there in that apartment. The guy gave me an offer, and I took it. He said he'd cut Rosy off, but only if I agreed to be at his beck and call if and when he needed me. I tried telling him I wasn't a criminal lawyer. Wouldn't he be better off with someone from that part of the bar?

He said he didn't care. Told me my coming here like this was enough for him. And he clearly liked the idea of some big-deal law firm in his corner.

I had to give him my word that I'd be there for him the minute he needed me. And for no charge. Then I could tell my brother to stand down. In addition to cutting Rosy off, neither the dealer nor any of his crew would go looking for Sean. That was part of the offer. There would be no preemptive strike on my brother, he told me, though not in those exact words.

When I got Sean far enough away from the apartment building, I told him all this. Well, not exactly in those words either.

I just told him that I had somehow managed to convince the dealer to stop selling heroin to Rosy.

Sean was still hot. And high. He started arguing, saying, "It's too goddamn late. The motherfucker is going down." He settled after a while.

And how was I going to explain to my law firm that I had agreed to undertake the legal representation of some scumbag drug dealer? And for free?

I wasn't. I'd keep that to myself and hope for the best. I did tell Diane as she stood at her kitchen counter buttering her bagel. She chuckled, wondering out loud if the day would come when she and I would be at opposite trial tables as she prosecuted and I defended the dealer and his crew. "Yeah, wouldn't that be a barrel of laughs?" I was saying when my phone pinged.

I had sent Jeremy and Gloria to India. Their mission was to go to Dipak Singh's law office and gather and review documents for shipment to Dunn & Sullivan.

India was nine and a half hours ahead of New York, so 11:30 a.m. in New York and 9:00 p.m. in India. Even though it was Sunday night there, Dipak's office told them that he personally would meet them at the airport, drive them into town to their hotel, get them settled, and then work out arrangements to meet with him at his office first thing Monday morning.

I read the e-mail. They were at the airport.

Dipak was a no-show.

23.

Peter Moss didn't wait.

Discovery or no discovery, he filed his complaint naming Dunn & Sullivan as a defendant. And he added an additional defendant: the hedge fund that Carl Smith had gotten to put up the money to finance the case for our law firm. Moss had learned of their existence in the few records we'd produced by that point. Peter Moss claimed that the hedge fund had to be in on the fraud. His reasoning?

Simple.

He claimed no way would they have ponied up legal-fee money for us without first carefully vetting the case. Since they put up the dough, they had to know. (A variation on the O.J. trial's "If [the glove] doesn't fit, you must acquit.") Moss pled this "on information and belief," of course.

Now that my law firm had actually been sued, I called Carl Smith's office like the good boy that I was. No e-mails or other writings from me. I knew how to follow orders. I was, after all, a team player. Like I said, not actually "one of the boys," but I suited up in the same locker room they used.

I called his secretary, told her what had happened. I mean, this was big. A venerable law firm like Dunn & Sullivan actually sued. And accused of fraud. The *New York Times* would be all over this. Carl was going to want to see me ASAP. Of course he was.

I got an e-mail.

An e-mail? After all that shit I took from him about my writing one fucking little e-mail. *Nothing in writing. You want me? You pick up the phone and call me.* Admonishing me, pointing his luncheon fork in my face like the drug dealer had with his silver pistol. And *he* sends *me* an e-mail?

Here it is.

To: Carney Blake
From: Carl Smith
Subject: GRE Amended Complaint

Mr. Blake:

As the partner in charge of the above-referenced matter, you have assured me there is absolutely no merit to any of the claims recently asserted against this law firm. It is imperative that you continue to take all necessary steps to clear this firm's good name and protect it from such frivolous allegations.

Carl Smith
Partner & Chairman
Dunn & Sullivan, LLP
One Times Square
New York, NY 10036

I was fuming. I put my fingers to the keys of my laptop and quickly banged out a response. A hot response. My index finger hovered over the SEND button as I proofread the e-mail. I mean, there was shit you didn't have to eat. Sauce for the goose was sauce for the gander. (I think I came up with another two or three wise old adages. Do unto others . . . and so on.) My index finger actually touched the SEND key. Then I hesitated. Send?

If you're thinking damn right send, fine. But you're standing at the sidelines. You know there's more to this story. I was in the moment. So.

I didn't. Simple as that. I went for Door Number Two. I walked down the hall to Anka Stankowski's office.

I was seated across from her, waiting as she read the complaint I had handed her. Every so often she would look up at me, then go back to reading. When she finished, I handed her the hard copy I had printed out of Carl Smith's e-mail. She read it and chuckled.

Still snickering, Anka leaned into her chair, the metal underpinnings groaning from her shifting girth.

"News flash, Carney Blake," she said. "Our Carl didn't get to be chairman of this firm by accident. He's a slick son of a bitch, protecting his ass at your expense."

You know, I really liked Anka. There was something very refreshing in her candor. She was the real thing. Big and fat and grotesque as she was, here was someone in my corner. What I saw was what I got. No pretense. No airs.

"Okay, so now what?" I asked.

"You wanna know your next move?" Anka asked.

"Yeah."

"Think about it."

I cleared my head and sat there thinking.

"Rule 11?" I said.

"Bingo."

Rule 11 was in the Federal Rules of Civil Procedure. Here's what you did:

First you wrote to opposing counsel telling him that he needed to withdraw his claims against Dunn & Sullivan because the allegations were frivolous and had nothing to support them. Then, when he refused, you served him with a motion for sanctions under Rule 11.

And dig this? You get to name not only the individual lawyer for misconduct but his entire law firm as well. This was good. I would be able to name Peter Moss's law firm for wrongdoing just like he had named mine.

What kinds of sanctions were we talking about?

Big ones: a substantial fine, a (verbal) bitch slap from the judge, and a removal of the troublesome allegations. And that would cripple the complaint against Dunn & Sullivan.

Yeah, that was the next move. Discovery had just begun. Whatever Peter Moss had, it couldn't be much. Moss had fired too soon, was too far from his target, with no real ammunition to hit it.

"And the hedge fund?" I asked, explaining that I myself had only just learned about its existence while reviewing documents we were producing in discovery. Anka shrugged.

"File your sanctions. Let their lawyers handle their own client. They'll likely piggyback onto your Rule 11 motion. Stay away from them. Deal with your shit, let them deal with theirs."

It was time for me to start drafting.

"Thanks," I said as I stood.

"Anytime."

An hour or so later, I had a technical question about how to plead one of the points I was making in my motion. I called Anka. It was just a quick question, no need for a visit. I got her secretary.

"She's out of the office at the moment," the secretary told me.

"When will she be back?" I asked.

"She won't be long," she said. "She's in with the chairman."

Huh?

24.

No grass grew under Carl Smith's feet either.

He knew that the *New York Times* was about to break the story of the fraud suit against Dunn & Sullivan. It would be the lead article in the paper's business section. He'd been tipped off. The paper's managing editor had called with a heads-up. They'd been undergraduates at Yale, and then later both had been elected to membership in New York's exclusive and stuffy Union Club, where they were intermittent squash partners. The story wouldn't change. The *Times* would run it as is. But the tip-off was part of the deal, the social compact among the elite.

So while I sat at my desk composing a sanctions motion, Carl was in with his IPO bankers for a little prepublication chat. They had obviously seen the earlier story in the Sunday *Times* about Big Law's "weight loss." He knew they needed to hear from him in advance of the upcoming *Times* article about Dunn & Sullivan and the fraud lawsuit. Trading in the law firm's stock, when actually issued, was expected to be high. So were the bank's fees. Still, a fraud suit on the eve of the IPO was troublesome.

Carl would play hide the ball with his bankers. What Carl wouldn't know was that they were playing hide the ball with him as well. They had secretly videotaped the meeting. It would later be entered into evidence.

Here's a reprint of that part of the transcript I'm talking about. It starts about ten minutes into the meeting. The bank's CEO has just asked Carl if there was any danger that the new lawsuit would unravel the IPO, especially in light of the earlier general article.

> **Carl:** No. None at all. Dunn & Sullivan is financially sound. You've seen our books. Seen the lucrative cases we've got stacked up like jumbo jets nose to tail on a busy runway. This new complaint? It's nothing. I have one of our best litigating partners on it. The court will throw it out for the piece of crap that it is.
>
> **Bank CEO:** Are you sure, Carl? To state the obvious, this IPO of a major law firm is a huge undertaking. A new frontier will be opened in the financial marketplace. There's lots of money to be made here. So, Carl, we are relying on you. You need to be sure. Are you?
>
> **Carl:** (*ducking the question*) Of course you're relying on me. And I want you to. Just as I'm relying on my very experienced law partner who's in charge of this case. He has assured me, and now I'm assuring you.
>
> **Bank CEO:** Fine, totally understandable. But, Carl, we're sitting with you. We've known each other . . . what? Fifteen years? Longer, come to think of it?
>
> **Carl:** Longer. Though you've aged more.
>
> **Bank CEO:** (*laughing*) You may be right about that. (*turning serious again*) But, Carl, you're the guy here as far as we're concerned. Not your partner. You need to look us in the eye and tell us there are no problems here. You understand, don't you?
>
> **Carl:** Absolutely. And I can and do assure you. Best I know. There is absolutely no problem.

Bank CEO: Great. Really appreciate that. But when you say
   "Best I know," you're not qualifying your assurances, are you?

The video shows Carl tightening the otherwise perfect knot on his necktie, twisting his neck ever so slightly. Later a body-language expert will testify that those are the signs of someone about to tell a lie.

Carl: No qualifications intended.

Bank CEO: Good to hear. So the IPO is still on green light.
   Now, Carl, what are you gonna do with all that money you're
   about to make?

(*Laughter all around the table.*)

A few days after Carl's bank meeting, Jeremy and Gloria returned to New York from India with the documents they had selected in tow. Most everything was in English, the GRE documents that Dipak had procured as well as the Indian court proceedings. English is the official language of the law in India. Given the twenty-two diverse ethnic languages recognized in India's constitution, there was no apparent alternative.

There was nothing in what my guys saw or brought back that showed any wrongdoing on Dipak's part, or on the Indian trial judge's for that matter. That was helpful. They never got to see Dipak. He hadn't set foot in his own law office the entire time they were there.

The guy needed to be seen. Anka was right.

And speaking of Anka. She called me back. I asked her point-blank had she said anything to Carl when she met with him.

"Listen," she said, her voice rising in anger. "If I say you can trust me to keep your confidences, then you can trust me to keep your confidences. If that's not good enough, you can go fuck yourself. Don't come by again."

She was about to hang up on me. I apologized. Anka said nothing. It was awkward. Both of us on the line, Anka pissed and me embarrassed. To fill up the dead air, I told her about Jeremy and Gloria's trip to India. And Dipak's disappearing act.

"Call him. E-mail him. Send him a fucking letter," Anka said. "Tell him he doesn't meet with you? You drop the case."

"Can I do that? I mean, this is the law firm's case, not mine alone."

"It's your case, Carney. Time for you to own up to it."

25.

I did.

Own up to it, I mean. I e-mailed Dipak Singh and also sent him a DHL Express–delivered letter. In no uncertain terms, I advised him that he needed to come to New York and meet with me "without further delay," or I would dismiss the GRE case.

That got me a call. But not from him.

"Hold for Mr. Smith," his secretary said after I picked up the phone.

I waited a good three to four minutes before Carl got on the line. I held. I would have liked to hang up and force him to call me again, but I swallowed my pride and waited. When he did get on—surprise, surprise—no greetings, right to business.

"What are you doing with that Indian lawyer?" he asked. There was no mistaking his annoyance.

"What am I doing?"

"It's not a difficult question, Blake."

"I'm trying to meet with him."

If I had to pick a time and place where I first began to think that something was really off here, I'd pick that call. The firm's chairman—keeping me at arm's length until now—wanting to crawl into my case?

"You've sent your associates to him. They've returned with his documents. I would think that should be sufficient."

Do you, now? I was thinking. *And how did you know about Jeremy and Gloria going to India? Did some dapper subcontinent lawyer reach out to you after getting my e-mail and/or letter?*

"Please don't take this the wrong way," I told Smith. "But you put me in charge of this case. And that's what I'm doing. I need to see this guy. It's simply imprudent for me not to under the circumstances."

"Imprudent?"

That did it.

"If you'd like, Carl," I said, "I'd be happy to prepare a detailed memorandum about where we are on this matter, what the problems seem to be, and where I think we need to go. I could have that on your desk before the close of business today."

He hung up on me.

Okay, now what? Run to Anka? Call Smith back and try to iron out whatever needed ironing out?

Or simply leave it be. Do nothing.

And that's what I did. Nothing.

Three hours later I received an e-mail from the ever-elusive Dipak. It was the middle of the fucking night in India, but the guy sends me an e-mail. Wonder how that happened?

Here it is:

My dear Mr. Carney Blake,

It is my understanding that you are desirous of meeting me. I would

be only too happy to present myself to you for that convivial

opportunity. However, it is also my understanding that, with the

pendency of litigation in New York, I could be subpoenaed to give testimony were I to present my humble self within the borders of your country.

Thus, I would be honored to meet with you at the Four Seasons Hotel, Hamilton Place, Park Lane, London W1J 7DR on Tuesday next. Please allow me the courtesy of your prompt reply.

Yours faithfully,
Dipak Singh
Law Offices Dipak Singh
27 Mahatma Ghandi Road
Guwahati, Assam, India

(Mahatma Ghandi Road is to India, I think, what MLK Boulevard is to America.)

My prompt reply followed.

Dear Dipak:
It's a date. I suggest lunch on Tuesday in the hotel dining room at 12:00 p.m.
Please confirm.

Regards,
Carney Blake
Partner
Dunn & Sullivan, LLP
One Times Square
New York, NY 10036

He didn't respond, didn't confirm. Radio silence. Was he going to stand me up like he did Jeremy and Gloria? Should I write him again and press for a confirmation? If I did that and he again didn't respond, then what? No, I had a better idea. A surer way to put his ass in my presence.

I sent another e-mail.

Hi, Carl:

Mr. Singh has e-mailed me and offered to meet in London on next Tuesday. I e-mailed him that I'd be there and have arranged for a luncheon meeting at the Four Seasons hotel at noon on that day. Just wanted you to know.

Regards,

Carney Blake

Partner

Dunn & Sullivan, LLP

One Times Square

New York, NY 10036

Then it was back to business.

I had finished the Rule 11 sanctions motion and had also sent the obligatory letter (it was by e-mail) to Peter Moss, demanding that he withdraw the Dunn & Sullivan complaint because the allegations were "frivolous and without any basis in fact" (that's the phrase the courts used in the cases I read while preparing the motion). I got this long, meandering e-mail back. It took up two full pages when I printed it out. What it said in socially acceptable lawyer's jargon was that I could go fuck myself. Nothing would be withdrawn.

I vetted my draft motion with Jeremy, who made changes that tightened the pleading considerably. Man, was he good. I also sent the draft to Anka. I don't think she actually read it. She turned it around too quickly, her one-word, hand-scribbled note saying only "Fine." (I kept that business with Carl Smith to myself. Didn't share it with her.)

Then I filed the sanctions motion under Rule 11.

I think it's fair to say that Peter Moss had upped the ante by bringing a separate case against Dunn & Sullivan. Anka got me to the right place, helped me figure out the next step. Now I had made that next step. I mean, two could play at this game. He had taken a swing at my law firm. I had just taken a swing at him and his law firm.

What did Moss do?

He sued me.

26.

Jeremy and I were on a British Airways red-eye flight.
We left JFK around dinnertime and were due to arrive at Heathrow the next morning London time. Jeremy was with me for a reason. I didn't want to meet with Dipak alone. I wanted a witness. In case.

We were booked in business class. On BA that gets you a flat-bed seat. Drinks and dinner had been served, the cabin lights dimmed. My seat was all the way back in the bed position. I was on my side with the blindfold on from the little travel pack each passenger got, trying for a couple of hours' sleep before we landed. The next day was sure to be hectic. Jeremy and I were booked back to New York late in the afternoon following our lunch meeting with Dipak. So no need even for a hotel room.

The plane's jets were droning, the cabin was filled with sleeping passengers. But not me. Couldn't sleep. My stomach was churning. By suing me, Peter Moss had put *my* skin in the game. I was now a named defendant alongside Dunn & Sullivan. *It's a ploy*, I kept telling myself. *Keep your eye on the ball; don't let Peter Moss trick you into swinging at the wrong pitch.*

I think I actually did sleep a little, because I was startled when the cabin lights came back on and the flight attendants appeared in the aisles with juice, coffee, and breakfast trays. Jeremy was already up. Had he slept any?

We landed quickly and in no time were parked at the gate, the seat-belt sign was switched off, and we made our way to fast-track customs and immigration (a BA business-class perk).

No need for a visit to the baggage carousel. We had only the brief-cases we'd carried on. So we walked to the lounge in the arrivals hall (another BA perk), where we showered, shaved, and had our suits pressed. Then it was on to the Heathrow Express train to central London, and before we knew it, Jeremy and I walked into the Four Seasons Hotel at Park Lane. It was 11:15 a.m. London time. The weather was colder and damper than what we'd left in New York, but we wouldn't be outside except to get on a train or into a cab.

We sat in the lobby and waited for Dipak to show up. Assuming he did.

"Pardon. Mr. Blake?"

I opened my eyes. Jeremy and I had been seated side by side on a lobby sofa, and I guess we'd dozed off. An elegantly dressed young man was standing before us with his head cocked like he was at the zoo trying to make out the nature of the species behind the glass enclosure.

"Dipak?" I said, rising to shake hands. His grip was fragile, his hand cool. But he was smiling, friendly.

Jeremy stood as well.

"This is my colleague Jeremy Lichtman from our New York office," I told Dipak as they, too, then shook.

"So, gentlemen," Dipak said, rubbing his hands together like he couldn't be more pleased to be in our presence. "May I escort you to the dining room? I have booked a table. It was for two, but no matter."

Dipak led the way. The hotel's Amaranto Restaurant was empty.

It seemed that noon was on the early side for lunch here. The maître d' showed us to a table. The room was all violently red-upholstered chairs with black-lacquered trimmings. More bordello than I would have expected from a five-star hotel. We took our seats, and immediately a waiter appeared.

We studied our menus, small-talked, ordered. My body clock told me it was the middle of the night, so I asked for an omelet, thinking that might work. Jeremy had only toast and coffee. It turned out Dipak was a vegetarian, so he ordered accordingly. We quickly finished our meals. It was time now to get down to business.

Dipak had been cordial throughout, though there was this distinct sense of noblesse oblige about him. Not that he was speaking down to Jeremy and me, but there was no mistaking the air of privilege and superiority wafting off this very young guy like thin mist off melting ice. He was polished, even elegant-looking with that fashionable stubble beard, the expensive suit, and so on. I think at first I might have subconsciously given him more credence than he deserved.

That didn't last long.

I had asked Dipak to take Jeremy and me through the case, how it had been prepared by him, and how it had been tried. And he did, at length. When Dipak got to the expert reports that he told us the judge found very persuasive, I stopped him.

"Dipak," I said, "there is an allegation that you wrote the report for the expert and submitted it to the judge as though your expert had written it, not you."

This was the first what I'd call "probing" question. Dipak's demeanor instantly changed. I could see him stiffen.

"I have already vetted this with your firm chairman. All was aboveboard. Of that I can assure you, good gentlemen."

"Fair enough," I said, "but, Dipak, we need to get into the weeds with you."

"Into the what?"

He knew goddamn well what I meant.

I nodded to Jeremy, who pulled out a sheaf of papers. He handed them to Dipak, who took them and didn't so much as glance at them before trying to hand them back to Jeremy.

"Hold on to them please, Dipak," I told him.

"Yes, okay," he said as Jeremy pushed them back toward him.

I watched Dipak shoot his cuffs. His wrists and the backs of his hands were matted with dark hair. Was that a nervous tic in his right eye? He still wouldn't look at the papers now resting by his forearm.

Jeremy and I exchanged glances.

"We got that stuff from your files," Jeremy told him. "They're drafts of the expert's report. Written by you, I think. The one on top of the pile is word-for-word identical to the official expert report you submitted to the judge in the case."

"No, I assure you," Dipak said, his gaze flicking between Jeremy and me. "That is not so."

"It sure looks like it to me," Jeremy said. I watched Jeremy's eyes drill into Dipak. This kid will be some trial lawyer when he gets more experience. You could just see it.

Dipak then rambled on about how what Jeremy had shown him wasn't his attempt to write the entire report for his expert. What he was saying was pure gibberish.

Quite frankly, a good answer would have been along the lines of Dipak's having presented a draft report to his expert, who then openly accepted it as representative of what he was going to tell the court anyway, and so he had adopted it as his own. But Dipak didn't say that.

Jeremy reached back into his briefcase and removed copies of some pages from Dipak's law-firm ledger, which he and Gloria had gotten on their visit to his offices.

With a quick glance my way. *Okay to go on?*

Go, I signaled.

"Mr. Singh," Jeremy said. "Take a look at these ledger pages. They seem to show that you presented several checks for rather large sums of cash just days before the GRE case was set to begin. What did you need all that cash for?"

"You are asking me for such detail, Mr. . . . ?"

"Lichtman."

"Lichtman. You cannot expect me to recall such detail, but I assure you that the transactions in question can be explained by my bookkeeper." Here he grimaced, clucked his tongue. "I do not know such detail."

"Was it for the judge?"

"The judge?"

"The judge."

"Certainly not."

"You sure?"

"Quite."

Dipak's eyes were now ricocheting between me and Jeremy. We watched as he removed his napkin from his lap and very carefully folded it into quarters. He told us he needed to make a quick trip to "the gents'," as he put it. He stood and headed for the restrooms out in the hotel lobby.

Jeremy and I waited.

And waited.

Once it was clear that Dipak wasn't coming back, I called for the check. When it arrived, I asked the waiter to put the charge to Mr. Singh's room. He left with the bill, then quickly returned to tell us that our luncheon host was not registered as a guest at the hotel.

And so it was back onto the Heathrow Express and the airport.

I sent Anka a text before boarding our flight, asking if we could meet first thing the next morning.

27.

Anka had her meaty fist around one of those thirty-one-ounce Starbucks Trenta iced coffees.

She heard me out about the London trip. I told her Jeremy and I came back with no real proof of fraud but that, to put it mildly, Dipak was evasive. And then there was his disappearing act.

I fully expected Anka to confirm my thinking. To say, *That's it. Time to shit-can the case. With or without Carl Smith's consent.* But that's not what she said.

Instead she asked, "How confident are you about the underlying case? Was the plant explosion badly handled? Did those Indian workers and their families really suffer?"

"It was, and they did," I told her. "And yeah, I'm confident."

Anka picked up her Trenta. I watched her drain it, then search for a remaining drop or two in the cup's bottom. Nothing. She had this profound look of disappointment as she dropped the cup into her trash basket.

"Then you gotta do what you gotta do," she said as she removed a vending-machine pastry from a desk drawer, delicately unwrapped the cellophane, and ate it in two humongous bites.

"Meaning?" I asked as Anka stifled a delicate burp.

"Come on, Carney. Do you represent that fancy-pants Indian kid lawyer or the people whose lives were fucked beyond repair by this mega-company's gross negligence and complete disregard for its workers and their families?"

Anka was right. The underlying case—no matter what happened at trial—was airtight. Worthy of redress, as we lawyers say.

But I was stumped.

"How do I do that?"

"You tell the New York judge you don't give a rat's ass about the Indian judgment. Fuck that. You'll ignore it. Instead you'll file a whole new case in her court. And you'll try it in front of her. Let her be the judge. Let her decide for herself if GRE ruined your clients' lives. Put it on her. She'll like that."

I shook my head no. Won't work.

"That tells the judge we had to know the Indian judgment was bad. And yet we relied on it in our asset-seizure case before her. That's what Peter Moss has sued our law firm"—I decided not to add *and me personally*—"for doing. We'd be handing Moss a judgment against us on a silver platter."

Anka thought for a moment.

"You're right," she said, stifling another belch. I pretended not to notice.

We sat and stared at each other. Anka's phone rang. She let it go to voice mail. Anka drumming those bratwurst fingers on her desk. Thinking. Then the gleam in her eye. Smiling and nodding.

"A shadow case," she said.

"A what?"

"A shadow case. You don't file a new case. You ignore the Indian judgment. You put on the case you can't bring in the case you *are* bringing. Even though you haven't pled it. Do you see?"

"Not yet."

Anka didn't seem impatient with me. She waited a beat for my thinking to catch up with hers. Then she continued.

"In the asset-seizure case you're trying, you put on the other case. You show the judge exactly what GRE did and didn't do and how that harmed your clients. She sees that the case is good. Is righteous. No matter what your dandy disappearing lawyer did or didn't do in India. Get your own fresh experts to look at the case. Get their reports. Show the judge she doesn't need to rely on anything put into evidence in the Indian case."

"Right, right. And so she sees she can comfortably order the asset seizures."

Anka still nodding. Animated. Exuberant. Really into it, I thought.

"Yeah. She does the needful. Rights a wrong. Then you've got your U.S. court precedent. Then you can use that in other jurisdictions to get more seizure orders. Relying on her. Fuck whatever happened in India. You're protecting your injured clients. Getting them what they're entitled to and never impugning the integrity of Singh."

I liked this. It was squarely in line with what I had decided that Sunday morning at Diane's. My job was those injured people. No soapbox necessary. I was their lawyer. It was my duty to protect them. Simple as that.

Back at my own desk, I turned to my laptop and began pecking away at an outline of how to put the shadow case together. I had barely started when a new e-mail came in. It was the latest from something called Law360, one of several subscription law newsletters the firm gives all its lawyers access to.

I casually read through the printed list of news items and then stopped. Third item down.

Dunn & Sullivan's entire antitrust section had defected. And to where?

Mason Rose. Peter Moss's law firm. At first that made no sense.

Peter Moss had sued our firm for fraud. And now he was stealing away our entire antitrust section?

This was like a corporate raid, I was thinking. No, wait. This wasn't *like* a corporate raid. This *was* a corporate raid.

Another penny dropped.

I'm pretty sure I would have run with that. Trying to see what Peter Moss was really up to, but I sensed someone standing in my open doorway. I looked up. It was my brother, Sean.

"How'd you get in?" I asked, surprised. "Reception didn't stop you?"

I saw the look on his face.

He shut the door.

28.

I looked down into the open grave at my father.

He was frantically trying to crawl out after he had drunkenly fallen in, a gash visible in his forehead where he hit the coffin on his way down.

"Bluddy hell, get me the fook outta here!" he screamed as I and a few other mourners knelt at the grave site and pulled my father back to the land of the living. Blood was cascading down his face.

My brother didn't move. He was in a trance.

Rosy was inside that coffin.

She had promised to stay away from the heroin dealer. But she was an addict, so she didn't. Maybe the dealer had kept his word to me. Maybe he hadn't. Who knows? Addicts are resourceful when it comes to their next fix. Rosy copped. From him or some other dealer. Didn't matter now. Sean had cut off what money there was. So Rosy hit the streets. Turned tricks. And that, not the drug itself, was what had killed her.

My father was back on dry land. He was still wobbly. Someone had given him a hankie he now had pressed to his forehead. He kept removing it and examining the bloodstains.

Just a few moments earlier, as the priest was sprinkling holy water and saying the blessing over Rosy's coffin, my dad, who had come late—and very drunk—started wailing. His hands in the air, his legs wobbling, he ranted on about poor Rosy. Not making any sense, really. Just going on like the drunk he was. He took one step too many toward the open grave, twisted around, and in he went.

Rosy's death was gruesome. She had gotten into the wrong car. The john had driven her out to Brooklyn's Sheepshead Bay area, not far from run-down Coney Island. After Rosy did what he wanted, the guy took out his wallet to pay. Rosy drew a knife on him, told the guy to hand over the wallet. They fought, struggling over the knife. It wound up stuck in Rosy's neck. She bled to death as the guy sat next to her in the car, paralyzed with fear and remorse.

He was a middle-class family man. Lived in Scarsdale and worked at some boring job in the city. He sat in the car panicked as Rosy bled out. Eventually a passing patrol car came upon them. The cop at the wheel shone his flashlight into his car. And that was that.

I looked at my brother. Our eyes met, and then he abruptly looked away. I kept my eyes on him. Saw his hurt. He was crushed. But he was also in a rage. Not good, I remember thinking.

Not good at all.

29.

B ack in court.

    But that afternoon I was the spectator watching Diane in criminal court at 100 Centre Street, a downtown stone's throw from the federal court where I'd spent the morning. I had slipped unnoticed into the back row of the courtroom. Scattered around the spectators' section were several young black men, a heavy-set black woman, and in the front row a skinny white guy in a cheap suit. He had to be from the pretrial-services office, waiting for the case to end with its inevitable conviction of the two defendants for a drug-related murder.

One of the defendants was on the stand, testifying in his own defense, contrary, no doubt to strongly worded advice from his defense lawyer *not* to do this. Diane was in the middle of her cross-examination. It was late afternoon, not long, I figured, before the judge would bring the proceedings to a close for the day.

"So let me see if I've got this right," Diane was saying as she stood at the podium located in the space between the two counsel tables. "You're saying you can't be held responsible for the death of Evander

Washington because you were there at the time of his murder, but just as a . . . what? A spectator?"

I watched the defendant, trying unsuccessfully for sage, nodding in agreement. (He also seemed incapable of suppressing his appreciation for Diane and so was very visibly clocking her. You could see it even with his wandering left eye weirdly pointing to where the jury was seated. This was not lost on the jury.)

This twenty-something street tough, dressed in going-to-court civvies rather than the orange jumpsuit with "DOC" (Department of Corrections) stenciled on the back that he no doubt had worn over here from the Tombs, where he'd most probably spent the better part of a year waiting for his case to be heard. He was dark-skinned and sinewy, with thick, bulging veins on his forearms. His hair was tight and sharply razored in a precise arc on his forehead and down his tiny arrowhead sideburns.

"Yeah, yeah," he told Diane (still one-eyeing her), nodding. "I be like there, know what I'm sayin'? But I dint do nothin'."

"Uh-huh," Diane said. I saw her glance over at the jury. Giving them the look. One of the jurors in the back row, an elderly Asian man, smiled at her, having a good time watching these two moron defendants take themselves down for the count.

"So you admit that you and Mr. Carter, the other defendant, sitting over there"—pointing—"met with Evander Washington in that deserted playground off 187th Street on the night in question?"

"Yeah. Uh-huh. Me and him was there."

"And you were there to assist Mr. Carter in selling drugs to Evander Washington."

I watched the defendant vigorously shake his head no.

"Na, na. Now, that ain't right. I wasn't sellin' no drugs."

"Mr. Carter was."

"I don't know nothin' 'bout that."

"But you were there?"

"Yeah, lady. I already said I was."

"You saw Mr. Carter hand several vials filled with a white powdery substance to Evander Washington and then get some money back from him. Right?"

The defendant shrugged. Getting bored with this. Losing interest.

"Maybe I seen that. But like I said, I don't know nothin' 'bout no drugs. Anythin' coulda been in them whatchoucallits. . . ."

"Vials."

"Yeah."

"Okay. But you were standing there when Mr. Carter and Evander Washington had words."

"Had what?"

"When Mr. Carter and Evander Washington had words. You know, an argument."

"Yeah, I seen that."

"And they were arguing about the quality and quantity of the drugs Mr. Carter had just sold to Evander Washington."

"Like I said, lady. Don't know nothin' 'bout that."

"Well, you were there and saw Mr. Carter take out his pistol and bash Evander Washington repeatedly on his head and face? Even after Evander fell to the ground."

"I seen it. But I dint do it."

"You were standing pretty close, weren't you?"

Now really bored.

A shrug. Nothing more.

"You need to answer verbally, so the court reporter can get down what you're saying."

"Yeah."

"Yeah, you were close?"

"Yeah. Uh-huh."

"Close enough to have Evander Washington's blood sprayed all over you. Your face. Your clothes, as Mr. Carter beat him to death."

The defendant seemingly thinking back on that. I saw him grimace.

"Yeah," he said. "Ruined my damn shirt. Brand-new, too."

I saw one of the jurors shake her head in disbelief that this was what upset him. The judge shot her an admonishing look.

"And when you were arrested a short time later, there were some bills found in your pocket that had Evander's blood on them, too."

Another shrug. So what?

The judge then imposed himself, telling the defendant, "Answer out loud."

I watched the defendant look up and over to the judge. Glared at him. Wordlessly warning, *You best watch what you sayin' to me, Old School.*

The judge outglared him. Years of practice, no doubt. The defendant looked away.

"Yeah," the defendant then told Diane. "Yeah. But see." Now *he* was pointing at the other defendant sitting half asleep at counsel's table. "He owe me money. Know what I'm sayin'? But that ain't got nothin' to do with all this. That personal 'tween me and him. Got nothin' to do with no drugs."

"No further questions," Diane told the judge. No need for anything more.

The judge turned to the public defender. "Redirect?" he asked.

The public defender didn't even bother to rise. "No, Your Honor," he said with a futile wave of his hand. *What's the point?*

So the judge then turned to the jury and told them they were excused for the day. Adding that they shouldn't discuss the case with anyone and shouldn't read about it in the papers or watch anything about it on TV.

The bailiff told all to rise, and when they did, the judge left the bench, and as the two defendants, now reshackled, were led away, Diane turned to go back to her table for her case file. That's when she noticed me standing in the back row. She rolled her eyes at me with a *Can you believe this?* look.

As I waited for Diane to get her stuff, I couldn't help but think what a messy mix of the needless and the necessary happens in courtrooms day in and day out. Unless there was a loony on Diane's jury who refused to convict for reasons completely divorced from reality, a guilty verdict was a sure thing. So was all this just going through the motions? Superfluous? A waste of time and money?

No, not really. You get your day in court. Doesn't matter if you're some street hoodlum or some fat-cat corporation. That's by design: to protect the innocent more than simply to punish the guilty.

The GRE case was not anything like this cut-and-dried criminal case. But it, too, had that mix of needless and necessary. As I sat at counsel table in the federal courthouse earlier that morning before coming over here, waiting for our judge to take the bench, I knew that storm clouds were brewing. My case was still afloat, though the seas were about to shift from merely choppy to rough.

But I felt like I might have found my sea legs.

30.

She was full of her usual piss and vinegar.

"Now, look," Judge Belinda Brown was saying. "This is getting out of hand. I don't like the way these two cases are progressing. Too slow. Way too slow. Something isn't right here. I told you both last time heads were going to roll. What? You didn't think I meant it?"

Judge Brown glared down at Peter Moss and me through her unfashionable eyeglasses. Tongue-lashing lawyers seemed her default way of doing business.

The courtroom was empty of spectators. Moss's associate, Harold Kim, was seated beside him, just like last time, with that same smug look on his face. But unlike last time, Jeremy Lichtman was seated out in the gallery beside Gloria Delarosa.

Up here with me was a new lawyer who'd been hired from some other law firm to represent the hedge fund that had been added as a defendant in the Dunn & Sullivan fraud case. Seated beside him were two other lawyers hired from two separate law firms to represent Dunn & Sullivan and me. That's right, lawyers for lawyers.

But why two, one for Dunn & Sullivan and a separate one for me?

Two answers.

Number one is the clinical/professional answer: There is always the possibility, though theoretical only, of a conflict of interest developing between my interests and that of my law firm.

Number two is the strategic (real) answer: It would be easier to isolate me and feed me to the wolves if the same lawyer didn't represent me and my law firm.

I knew both answers but thought the "theoretical only"—at that point—was a part of them both. I called Anka about this.

Her response:

"How many times do I have to tell you, Carney? Keep your eye on the fucking ball. Don't worry about theoretical shit. How fucking hard is this for you to understand? Worry about your own fucking clients."

Then she hung up.

Anka's usual way with words.

So why were we all gathered there in federal court that morning?

Discovery was by then well under way, though far from completed. Things were indeed getting out of hand. Thanks to all the lawyering. Some would say overlawyering.

To review the bidding: Peter Moss had filed a motion to throw out my asset-seizure case against GRE. I had filed a Rule 11 sanctions motion against Moss for having brought his separate fraud case against Dunn & Sullivan. Then Moss sued me, too. This is new, but Moss also filed his *own* Rule 11 sanctions against me for having filed *my* Rule 11 sanctions against him. (Still with me here?)

And on and on and on. He filed this. We filed that. Everything under the sun was asserted by one side and objected to by the other. Big Law at its best. Or worst. The case was bogging down. Legal fees were hitting the roof.

The judge must have been monitoring this. Forests were being cut down to generate the mass of paperwork hastily written and even more hastily filed. So it was Judge Brown who had summoned us before her that morning. She was going to stop all this and put these two companion cases back on track. A fast track.

She was determined to get to that place where she could see who was doing what to whom without all this unnecessary maneuvering by the lawyers. But first she had her eye on me.

"Mr. Blake," she said.

I got to my feet.

"Your Honor?"

"Well, Mr. Blake," she said, "you are now no longer just a lawyer in this dispute."

"True, Your Honor."

"Don't you think it would be prudent for you to step away from the GRE case? Let some other lawyer handle it? How can you trust your judgment as an advocate when you're being accused of some pretty egregious conduct as a party in the other case?"

I didn't like the way she was looking at me.

The guy who was my lawyer started to rise. I saw it in his face (so far he'd spent all of five minutes with me) even before he uttered a single word. This milquetoast was about to try to appease the judge. At my expense. I waved him back down.

Remember, *fuck me once, shame on me* . . .

"No, Your Honor, I don't think it prudent for another lawyer to take my place. Can I tell you why?"

"I'm all ears, Counsel," she said, letting me know this better be good.

"Your Honor," I heard Peter Moss say as he rose to his feet. Ready to slip in an advanced barb or two at my expense.

I watched him button his suit jacket, then quickly glance down at Kim. *Watch this.* Now back up to the judge, with that toothpaste-commercial smile. *Hey, can I help out here, Judge?*

"The judge asked me, not you, so sit down," I told him, in what was a clear break from decorum. Counsel addresses the judge. The judge addresses counsel. Counsel do not address one another. Let alone issue orders to sit the fuck down.

Moss stayed on his feet, shaking his head in sad amusement. Who did I think I was, telling him to sit down? He looked over to the judge for reinforcement.

"You heard him. Sit down," the judge said.

"You Honor, before I—"

"Down, Counsel. Now."

Peter Moss retook his seat. I watched his smile fade. Kim stared off into deep space. No percentage in letting the boss know he'd overplayed his hand.

"Mr. Blake?"

"Yes, Your Honor," I said, ready for this, I thought. "This case isn't really about Indian trials and Indian judgments. And it most certainly isn't about me—"

"I'm not so sure I can agree with that," she interrupted. "Your entire case, your effort to seize assets, is in full reliance on that very Indian court judgment. And you are the lawyer using that judgment here in this court. Or I should say trying to. Don't you agree?"

"No, not really, Your Honor."

"How so?"

"You see—" was as far as I got before Moss sprang back up.

"Your Honor is absolutely—"

"One more word out of you, Mr. Moss, and I will hold you in contempt." As Judge Brown said this, she patted the air in front of her like Moss was an unruly pup in canine obedience school. "Down," she ordered again.

Moss said nothing. Retook his seat. Pissed. Kim was now busy studying the great seal up there on the wall high above the judge's head.

Okay, the judge liked that I had finally figured out how to lawyer. Still I told myself, *Don't push this too far.*

So, carefully choosing words, I told her how what really mattered here was what had happened to the plant workers and their families. That case was clear—solid, even—I told her. GRE was negligent, grossly so, and had caused all the damage and injury that was no doubt proved before the Indian judge and would be proved by me before her in the case we'd filed in this court. What might or might not have happened procedurally in the Indian court? Didn't matter, I said.

For some reason, as I said that, I shifted my gaze over to Moss and Kim. Both were glaring at me. And that told me I was doing something right here for once.

So I went on to tell the judge that this case was so clear I intended to bring in new independent expert witnesses directly to her, who would provide their opinions, untouched by legal hands, on GRE's outrageously negligent and wanton behavior.

"You make an interesting argument, Counsel," Judge Brown told me after I finished. "I'm not sure I buy it, but time will tell."

Then she turned to Moss. "Okay, Mr. Moss. Up. Let's hear it."

Moss stood. But something had changed. He seemed no longer interested in saying anything.

"As Your Honor said, time will tell."

Then he sat down.

Still on my feet, I watched him, saw something in his eyes. A flash. I think that was the moment Peter Moss realized I wasn't just some fumbling kid lawyer.

Then it was back to the lecture from the judge. She severely shortened the time period for us to finish discovery. She made us both agree on the record that we understood and would comply with her wishes.

"No further delay, Counsel. You got that?"

"Yes, Your Honor," Moss (back on his feet) and I sang in unison.

Then she dismissed us. And this time Moss didn't come over to me. Didn't treat me to his usual false bonhomie. He got up and walked out of the courtroom, leaving to young Mr. Kim the job of collecting his papers.

And I was feeling pretty good. Jeremy came over and patted me on the back. Nice job.

That's when I decided to take the rest of the day off. I treated myself to a couple of slices of thin-crust pizza. And then I walked over to the criminal courts to catch the afternoon session of Diane's drug-murder trial.

All good.

But Peter Moss was far from through with me.

31.

Peter Moss on the line.

He called first thing the next morning.

"What can I do for you?" I said.

There was a pause, and then.

"Actually," Moss said. "It's what I can do for *you*."

"Really?"

And then he surprised me.

"I'm prepared to drop you from the case. With prejudice."

I said nothing. There was clearly more.

"Here's the deal, Moss said. "You agree to testify for me at trial. Look, we both know whatever took place in India is fucked up. You testify that you didn't see it at first. Then you did. You resigned from your firm because they insisted on continuing with the case. And now you're making amends by becoming a witness for our side and confirming that fraud in fact did go on in the Indian case and that Dunn & Sullivan knew it then and knows it now."

"You've got to be kidding."

"Not in the least. And trust me, you'll be better off in the long run with a job in some other law firm. Maybe once this is over, I can even help you."

What Peter Moss was proposing was just not done. This wasn't some criminal case where the prosecutor cuts deals with some of the defendants to flip over and testify against other defendants in return for leniency. This was civil litigation. A commercial dispute. Not some . . . what? Drug-related murder trial.

"Quit my firm? What are you smoking?"

"I'm going to give you exactly two days to think this over," he said, pausing. Then adding, "You seem like a nice guy. I really don't want to hurt you. But listen, this won't end well for you if you don't take my deal. I can't go into detail. But get out now while you still can. You just need to trust me on this."

Trust him? He was my adversary, and he wanted me to trust him?

"I don't need two days. Or two minutes. Offer declined."

"Yeah, well, take the two days I'm giving you and think about it. Get some independent legal advice. Like I said, I don't want to hurt you. But I will if you get in my way."

"Your what?"

"Get some counsel," he repeated, then hung up.

I didn't run this by Anka. I'd been to that well too many times as it was. And I had no intention of discussing anything with the outside legal counsel Dunn & Sullivan got for me.

Besides, what was there to talk about? I remember thinking.

Moss was asking me to become his litigation bitch. That was all this was. Who in his/her right mind would do something like that?

On the third day, I got a package from Moss's office. Inside were new pleadings. The hedge fund had been dropped from the case as a defendant. With prejudice. And then had reentered the case as co-plaintiffs with Moss against Dunn & Sullivan and me. Their claim?

We had lied to them, as much by omission as commission. Had they known the truth about what had happened in India, they said, they wouldn't have put one red cent into the case, let alone the millions they'd invested for our legal fees on the strength of our assurances that what we had was a good, clean case.

In the package was also a copy of a letter Peter Moss had sent to the New York bar.

He had filed what was called a grievance against me. His intent, the letter said:

My disbarment.

32.

Shit. Fuck.

Those were the first two words of my notes from back then.

I just reread my notes from around that time. It triggered the same fist-to-the-stomach feeling, just as it did when I first wrote them. I thought again about Diane telling me this was just a job. That I needed to keep things in perspective. And of course that is exactly what I did *not* do. Bye-bye, sea legs.

I was entrenched in my first case as lead counsel. My firm's chairman was at best keeping me at arm's length and at worst playing me. I'd been sued, and now I was also facing a bar grievance proceeding where my license was in jeopardy. (And I hadn't even considered that I might also be indicted for criminal behavior, let alone put on trial.)

It was very clear from my notes. My take back then? This was all about me. And of course it wasn't all about me. In so many ways this wasn't about me at all. I was a small player in a much bigger game. But I was frightened and I was angry. A bad combination for a lawyer.

It was that kind of behavior that put my relationship with my girlfriend in the penalty box. (Tell you about that in a minute.) It also affected how I reacted to unfolding events. And, man, were there unfolding events. Some case-related, others simply the shit that happens.

Where to start?

The sequence doesn't really matter. So I'll begin with Carl Smith.

33.

New York was experiencing a premature temperature uptick.

It was early in the season, but we were in a mini heat wave. It wouldn't last more than a few days. Global warming, most everyone said. So Carl had broken out his spring suits.

He was feeling pretty good as he walked into his office that day all Brioni-ed up.

The Dunn & Sullivan IPO was at the starting gate. For Carl it was now a matter of when and no longer if. Sure, there were still a few wrinkles that needed ironing out. One in particular was going to cost him some serious money. *So what?* he thought. There was going to be a ton of money coming his way, and this latest snag was simply one of those costs of doing business. Nothing more.

So Carl was feeling pretty good. (The GRE case? No longer his problem. By the time it exploded, or imploded—if it did—Carl and his IPO would be a distant memory.)

Carl sat at his desk. His secretary had come and gone with his coffee and morning mail. He sipped at his coffee, leaving the mail unattended, catching up instead on e-mail. When finished, he next ran his eyes over the day's schedule. "Lunch at bank." Then he turned to his snail mail, flipping through it to see what might be important and what could wait.

The envelope had been marked "personal and confidential," and there was a layer of Scotch tape over the flap. No sender's name on it, just Carl's name and address, handwritten. His mind really elsewhere, Carl tore open the flap and then angled the envelope so that its contents could slide out.

The photos were eight-by-ten glossies. A series of them. Instinctively, Carl's brain slammed into lockdown, wouldn't admit into his consciousness what he was seeing. Two seconds later, the power back on and the gates back up, his hands started shaking. One of the photos slipped out of his grip and slowly sailed downward. Carl's heart was hammering a mile a minute. *Oh my God oh my God oh my God.*

Carl was on his knees trying to fish the escaped photo from under his desk where it had landed, lodging itself in a far corner. A clump of his hair rubbed itself out of place on the underside of the desk's center drawer. His phone was ringing, though it barely registered on him. It was the ringtone that signaled his secretary calling, no doubt with some routine reminder for him. The ring shut off, and a moment later came a knock on his door.

"Mr. Smith. Carl?" his secretary said as she carefully opened the door.

Carl was back on his feet, the renegade photo firmly in his grip but face out, its image directly within his secretary's line of vision. She looked down at it, then up at him and his wild hair, then down again, then up at him again. *What the . . . ?* her eyes screamed. Frozen, barely letting out breath, staring at the close-up of her boss with his boy toy in full Florida fellatio. Then at him, then down, then up. Not a word from either of them. Finally she managed to reverse gear and slowly back her way out of his office, closing the door so softly that Carl couldn't even hear the latch click.

Carl retook his seat. Stunned. "Shit. Fuck," he whispered to himself. (My very words.)

It wasn't often that Carl Smith lost it. Until that moment? Maybe never. He furiously tore the photos to pieces. Ripped them to shreds. Then what? Where to put them? He was having trouble breathing. Was he hyperventilating? He dropped the lacerated pieces on his desk. He retrieved the envelope, thinking he'd stuff them in there. That was when he noticed the note. He stuck his hand in and extracted it.

It was handwritten. Penned by Polly's divorce lawyer (you remember Iván the Impaler). It never did make its way into evidence, destroyed as it was by Carl along with the photos, but Iván Escobar later testified he remembered it word for short word:

"My office. Three p.m. today. Strongly suggest you be there."

The weather was just as out-of-season warm in Wallingford, Connecticut, as it was in New York.

Peter and his wife, Patricia, sat together in the small room provided for families at Wallingford's Gaylord Hospital, the one Josh had been rushed to after the accident and to where they had sped from Washington, D.C., after Peter had gotten the call.

The doctor had just left. The situation was not good.

A freak accident. Those were the headmaster's words when he'd called Peter at his law office. Josh had fallen through the window of an upper-floor dormitory at his boarding school.

Choate's campus was the picture-perfect setting for most anyone's notion of an elite boarding school. A patrician mini-world of gentle rolling hills and dynamically understated buildings, it was first among a handful of New England academies prepping the sons and daughters of affluent and noteworthy families (plus just enough minority schol-arshippers for cover) for the Ivy League majors. The boys' dormitory room was located in Hill House. Administrative offices were on the lower floors, dorm rooms on the floors above.

The boys were only horsing around good-naturedly, physically energetic, as young boys so often are. Peter's son just lost his footing as he and one of his floormates were locked in their approximation of a wrestler's grip.

A slight push backward, a slip on the polished wood floor. The kids were in underwear and socks. And out the window he went. No screams, just a free fall, the other kids momentarily stunned by the uncanny silence. No one in the lower-floor offices saw anything. But they heard the thump when Josh landed. They, too, later thought back on that eerie silence.

He had survived the fall, though he broke his neck. The doctor had told Peter and Patricia their son would most certainly live. But would he be paralyzed for life?

"Possibly, though hopefully not," the doctor had said.

Paralysis from a broken neck was not always permanent, he explained. And preliminary tests indicated that Josh's spinal cord, while badly bruised, had not been severed. That was a good sign. Time was needed, and recovery would be slow. In his experience, the doctor told Peter and Patricia, patients often regained some motor and mobility skills. Time would tell, he repeated, as he left them for his next scheduled surgery.

Moments after Peter had gotten off the phone with Josh's head-master and raced home to collect his wife for the drive up to Connecticut, the *New York Law Journal* reporter he had invited to meet with him that day got off the elevator and entered the lobby of Peter's law firm's reception area.

"Julia Grossman to see Peter Moss," she told the attractive and smartly dressed receptionist.

The receptionist provided the warm and welcoming smile she'd been instructed to deliver to all guests. If she took in this young reporter's disheveled appearance, lumpy body, and bad hair day, she hid it well. Instead, still beaming, she called down to Peter's office. And then, after a brief exchange with Peter's secretary:

"I'm so sorry, Miss Grossman," the receptionist told her, "but it seems that Mr. Moss has left for the day."

"No, that can't be right," said Ms. Grossman, instantly annoyed. "He invited me down from New York. We have a scheduled meeting." And then, with a quick glance at her oversize man's wristwatch, "In fact, it's to begin right now. So call again," she instructed the receptionist.

This young journalist was primed for anger at the least provocation. The *New York Law Journal* was the only job offer she'd gotten after graduate school. She had wanted better than that. She was better than that. She wanted the *New York Times*. And she was determined to write enough provocative stories to get their attention.

The receptionist did as she was told.

"I'm terribly sorry," she told Grossman once again. "But Mr. Moss has left for the day."

With that, the reporter turned on her heel and marched herself out of the firm's lobby.

Peter had indeed offered to meet with her, promising an exclusive story, so long as she didn't attribute it to him.

Julia Grossman had taped the call. Here's the salient part:

Grossman: But you're not denying that those people working at the Indian plant were injured, many of them fatally?

Moss: That's not the point, Julia. Bribing judges, falsifying evidence, and then using a court judgment to award a king's ransom to some greedy and corrupt lawyers. That's the point.

Grossman: And your proof?

Moss: Come down to D.C. and I'll prove it. Like I said, so long as you agree to keep my name out of it, I'll show you bank documents generating large amounts of cash. I'll show you everything.

Then, a little further on in the call:

Grossman: Say, listen, I don't have enough to write about this yet. But what have you heard about Dunn & Sullivan going public? That would be a first for an American law firm, wouldn't it?

Moss: Going what?

Grossman: Going public. An IPO? What have you heard?

On the tape there is a long period of silence. This was clearly the first that Peter Moss had learned about Carl Smith's plans. He was stunned. He needed to think this through.

Sands were shifting.

So when Peter finally spoke up, it was only to get off the call.

Moss: Why don't you come down here tomorrow around eleven? We can talk some more. I promise I'll show you what I've got. Answer all your questions.

Grossman: Okay. See you then.

And the call ends.

In a cab to Reagan National Airport and the Delta shuttle back to Manhattan, the reporter, iPad on her lap, began tapping out the story she was going to e-mail to her editor immediately after landing at La Guardia.

As far as she was concerned, there was only one explanation for

Moss's behavior. A change of heart. Cold feet. It had happened before. This wasn't the first time some source had blown her off. In fact, it was happening all too frequently these days. She was determined to show Moss (and hopefully the *New York Times*, if they ever started paying attention to her work) that there was a price to be paid for dissing this determined reporter.

She was going to teach Peter Moss not to fuck with the power of the pen. Julia Grossman pressed the RETURN tab on her virtual keyboard and began a new paragraph to broaden the scope of her story. Now she would have two targets.

Dunn & Sullivan.

And Peter Moss.

34.

Same day, 3:00 p.m.

Iván Escobar pointed to one of the low-slung easy chairs across from the nine-foot sofa where he was perched as his secretary ushered Carl into his office.

"Take a seat," he ordered Carl.

Iván's office was even more elaborate than Carl's, though not in the antique-mausoleum style Carl favored. Here everything was sleek, angled, and glossy. His front-door-size desk, set aslant at the room's other end, was all glass and steel, with neither a pen nor a sheet of paper anywhere in sight. A Hollywood studio head would kill for this office.

"Beatrice," Iván said to his secretary as she stood awaiting orders. She, too, was that fictive studio head's "casting couch" notion of an assistant: tall, flowing blond hair, copiously busted and stiletto-heeled, with legs up to her ears. She wore a navy-blue, thigh-high sheath that looked as if it had been meticulously painted onto her torso. "Please bring the gentleman something." Then, to Carl, "Coffee, tea?"

Carl shook his head. He didn't want coffee from this son of a bitch. What he wanted was to put his hands around the bastard's neck and slowly squeeze the life out of him.

"No?" Iván said, shrugging an *Up to you*. Then, to Beatrice, "Thank you, dear. That'll be all."

Iván took the time to watch his secretary's sultry exit. Once the door closed, he threw a mischievous wink in Carl's direction, purposefully ignoring Carl's scowl.

"So," Iván continued, as though nothing out of the ordinary was going on. "Let's get down to business, shall we?"

A fat beam of sunlight released from a covering cloud slowly bled its way across Iván's massive fiftieth-floor office, passing first over him and then Carl before once again disappearing behind a cloud. Iván waited as Carl sulked. I could just picture these two overdressed dandies in this Manhattan face-off. Eyeball to eyeball. High noon in New York City.

Then.

"Has my wife seen the photos?"

Iván nodded. "And the video, too. Didn't send that to you," he said, adding, "Want to watch it with me?"

Carl ignored that.

"Let me have the paper," he told the divorce lawyer.

Iván reached over to the glass side table by his elbow and picked up a copy of his list of demands. It was identical to the one Carl had ripped to pieces at their earlier meeting in Dunn & Sullivan's conference room.

He leaned forward, placed it on the low coffee table (also glass, of course), and once again slid it Carl's way.

"You know the drill, Carl," he said. "No changes. No deletions. Sign where it says 'Agreed.'"

Carl picked up the document. He reached inside his suit-jacket pocket and retrieved his reading glasses. He spent precious little time reading, then took a fat Montblanc pen from his jacket, laid the paper back on the glass table, and scribbled his signature.

"I'll have a more comprehensive divorce and settlement document prepared in due course," Iván told him.

Without another word Carl rose from his chair and walked out of the office.

By the time he'd made it down the elevator to the building's cavernous lobby, he was in an absolute rage. No way was this divorce lawyer ever going to let up on him. This was far from over. Carl could see that. He stood at the building's entrance deep in thought as crowds of New Yorkers rushed by.

Keep in mind Carl's fist was still holding on for dear life to that coconut.

The way to stop this wasn't with that asshole upstairs. No, that was a dead end. It was with that stupid alcoholic bitch of a wife. Her.

Desperate times called for desperate measures, Carl silently decided. He knew what he had to do.

But like they say, be careful what you wish for.

35.

Things not to say to your girlfriend:

Why is it so hard for you to understand? Or: *You call that helping?*

And yes, I said them. Am I sorry?

Oh, yeah.

So we were at dinner. Diane and me. That night we had made the pilgrimage to fashionable Williamsburg and were seated at one of those newish pop-up-style restaurants dotting this ultra-hip enclave's streets where postadolescent chefs gather a daily assortment of disparate ingredients and then hurl them into saucepans straddling leaping burner flames and perform culinary alchemy.

Despite my black mood, I couldn't believe the savory jolt of what I was eating. How did that scrawny kid-lady (ninety pounds soaking wet) in the restaurant's open kitchen, tattooed and pierced like some sideshow freak, do that? Unbelievable. On one side of my plate: prunes, peppers, and Kobe beef. On the other: turnips, essence of artesian beer, curded water-buffalo cheese, peppercorn-suffused bison-bacon bits.

Diane was toying with her vegetables (one or two I'd never even heard of), shifting her dinner from one side of the plate to the other as I droned on. I gulped down some more wine and then helped myself to the bottle resting between us. Imbibing in moderation? Fuck it. Instead I drained the last drop and, without asking if we should get another, raised and jiggled the empty at the guy who was serving us. He nodded okay from across the room but gave me that look I'm pretty sure waiters reserve for alcoholics.

In the last several days, I had been babbling nonstop.

When I look back, I see how utterly tone-deaf my whining had become. As I said, I was both frightened and angry. And feeling sorry for myself.

And, I was pushing Diane to the limit.

"I mean, give me a fucking break," I was telling her (again). "Why does all this have to be on me?"

Diane placed (slammed?) her fork on the table. She let out enough air to pump up a sagging tire. Shook her head.

"For crying out loud, Carney. Get a grip. If it's too much for you? Leave. Your law firm can easily find some other partner for the case. Go someplace else. No case is worth what you're putting yourself through. Get another job."

"You call that helping?" I said, sarcasm dripping from my words like oozings from a neglected wound. Shaking my head in mock agreement. "Oh, that's really helpful. Just throw my hands up in defeat and walk away. Then go and take some low-paying, low-stress law job. Like what? Become a prosecutor?"

Diane stared at me across the table as I reached for the new wine bottle.

"You think my job's so much less than yours? That I'm not as committed as you?"

I shouldn't have said what I'd said. I didn't even believe it. Remember, I'd seen Diane in court. She was good. Really good. And, like all busy, overworked, and underpaid prosecutors, she had an overflowing caseload. So did I apologize?

No. I drank instead.

And that's when I went for the *Why is this so hard for you to understand?* Right there.

Diane didn't respond. Well, not at first. She looked at me and kept looking. You know, I think I actually saw it in her eyes, could read her thoughts as precisely as if she'd written them in ink on the face of her linen napkin, which she was tossing atop her dinner plate. *That's it, Carney. That's it.*

"Good luck with your case," she said as she got up and walked out of the restaurant.

36.

This is embarrassing.

I wish I could portray myself throughout this story as some kind of lawyer action hero. But I faltered. I just did. To this day I'm uncertain exactly what got me to pull out of the deep end of that cesspool of self-pity into which I had so stupidly cannon-balled. But I did. And I was proud of that. No matter what happened afterward.

So, back on dry land, first things first: I called Diane's cell about a million times before she picked up. She said we needed a break. When a woman says that to a guy, "break" is spelled O-V-E-R.

I didn't push it. Told her I understood. Would she take my calls? Could we at least keep an open line?

"Carney," Diane said. (I heard the sigh.) "Look, we can always be friends. . . ."

When a woman says that . . . well, you know.

And that's how we left things.

But was Diane right? If I couldn't stand the heat, did I need to get out of the kitchen?

No.

There was no foolproof way out for me. I wasn't going anywhere. There were now two cases pending against me, one in federal court and the other before the bar. Damaging accusations had been leveled. People would remember the charges. Without a clear on-the-merits vindication, those charges would dog me throughout my career. I needed to see things through, stay in the game.

Heat or no heat, there I was. I just needed to be smarter. I needed to learn how to keep my head down when necessary and up when needed. I was in for the duration. At least that way I had a fighting chance. And there was this large class of Indian plaintiffs. Not one of them knew my name. But they were counting on me.

The *New York Law Journal* reporter who Peter Moss had stood up added in her two cents with an article about the GRE litigation and how a bunch of big-firm lawyers, on both sides, were papering the case to death and suing one another while no one seemed to care about the plant workers who'd been grievously hurt, and so on. Her article disclosed the disbarment proceeding pending against me that was supposed to be strictly confidential. No one ever discovered the source for that leak.

Meanwhile the slump that the country's top law firms were struggling through as their revenue stream kept dropping generated even more stories about the death of Big Law. Hallway gossip buzzed. A good deal of it fueled by worries that if the ships of the Big Law armada were taking on water, everyone on board was going down with them. It was an overreaction, but there was a kernel of truth there as well.

A sizable number of those law firms were laying off lawyers and staff, cutting hourly rates in a desperate attempt to keep clients, and merging with other law firms in the futile hope that two insolvent law firms combined would miraculously become one solvent law firm.

Big Law was indeed in trouble, but to paraphrase Mark Twain, the reports of its death were greatly exaggerated. So long as there was a corporate world and a Wall Street dangling big bucks, there would be top-tier, high-priced legal talent available. But there was clearly trouble brewing. Let's call it a Big Law "market correction."

And all the while Carl was busy cooking Dunn & Sullivan's books.

Here's a small slice of some more transcribed testimony. The person deposed was Dunn & Sullivan's chief financial officer. I say "was" because by the time of the deposition he had lost his job and had been unable to find another. I recently rewatched the video taken at the deposition. This CFO, some weasel in a suit jacket the same pale gray as his complexion, keeps mopping his brow with a paper towel handed him by his lawyer.

> **Deposing Lawyer:** So let me get this straight. You changed accounting entries. Turned some law-firm liabilities into assets, and simply wrote off others. All to make the firm look financially healthy when it really wasn't. You did all that so that the bank's underwriters would be fooled into believing that a pre-IPO Dunn & Sullivan was not only solvent but flush with money in the bank?
>
> **CFO:** (*mopping his forehead and then studying the wet and limp towel as though it might contain some magic disappearing potion*) I respectfully refuse to answer based on my Fifth Amendment rights against self-incrimination.
>
> **Lawyer:** How many times did you meet with Carl Smith about these book entries?
>
> **CFO:** I respectfully refuse to . . .

And that's how it went until the lawyer terminated the deposition.

To be clear, by that point the guy's nervous invocation of the Fifth wasn't to protect Carl. It was to protect himself. Carl might have directed the guy's actions, but they were his actions. When the CFO did what he did, he put himself on the hook. And Carl?

Carl was careful. Left no paper trail. Did whatever he did under the cloak of relying on the law firm's billing department and outside accountants for everything, professing that he really didn't understand all that paper-shuffling bookkeeping anyway. If these people did anything they shouldn't have? Well, that was on them.

Certainly not on him.

37.

"Big Law Eats Its Young.'"

"What?"

"That'll be the next headline."

That was Jeremy Lichtman to me. He had come to my office, purportedly to see if I'd read the legal research memos he'd e-mailed earlier in the day. But what he really wanted was to schmooze about all the recent Big Law bad press.

It was after 6:00 p.m., not even close to quitting time for many of those toiling up and down the cavernous halls on the various floors occupied by Dunn & Sullivan's midtown offices. I had read his memos, but it took very little time (seconds) for the two of us to slide off subject. I had moved my wastepaper basket from under my desk to the far wall. Not too far, actually, given the size of my office.

So Jeremy's in a chair at the foot of my desk, and I'm seated behind my desk, each of us with a DUNN & SULLIVAN–embossed legal pad on our laps, pulling off sheets one by one, crumpling them and then seeing how many we each could toss in the basket. Me? All but one so far. Jeremy? None.

"Eats its young?"

"Yeah," Jeremy said, tossing another crumpled ball wide of the basket.

"What the fuck does that mean?"

"Well," he said, "first the geniuses that run the big law firms start 'downsizing.' Cutting staff. Won't work. Revenue is too far down, expenses too far up. Next come the partners."

I sank another crumpled Dunn & Sullivan sheet. Jeremy's next shot bounced off the back wall and missed the basket by a good two feet. He shrugged and ripped off another page.

When Jeremy came into my office, he left the door open. Richard Miller caught my eye as he stormed down the hall. He didn't look my way, off to God-knew-what other skirmish. Jeremy didn't notice him, intent as he was on trying to make the next shot. He didn't.

Jeremy was on top of the GRE case. He was my wingman. I knew I could rely on him. And that certainly proved right. Still, for all that, Jeremy never really had *his* head in the game.

"Won't happen," I said. "Partners can't be fired."

"Yeah, it'll be a bitch." (Another shot, another miss.) "Here are all these best of the best lawyers who pissed away any kind of normal life in exchange for eight years of associate drudgery down in that coal mine. Then the few who actually make it come out and see just a glimmer of daylight before they're sent back down, though now with that unenforceable assurance of partnership tenure and just a slightly better life. And then," Jeremy said as he snapped his fingers, "poof, handed their walking papers." And then, mimicking management, "'Look, sorry. But you're a team player. Always have been, from the first day you set foot in here from Harvard or wherever, so you need to take one for the team. Good-bye and good luck.'"

"Won't happen."

"You think? All those set-for-lifers with their big incomes, big homes and cars, mortgaged no doubt to the hilt based on the assurance of all those anticipated years pulling down millions. The legal-fee faucet shrinks to a drip? They'll be gone faster than you can . . . sink another basket."

And I did.

"So why are you still here? You hate this life so much?"

Jeremy shrugged. Took aim with his latest crumpled sheet, then lowered his hand. He looked at me with that mischievous smile I bet he gave that Seven Dwarfs (Sleepy? Dopey?) partner years earlier when slow-motioning his explanation. Jeremy's outer shell displayed someone meek, spiritless. Nothing could be further from the mark. He chuckled.

"I'm in it for the training. And the inflated salary. I mean, where else can a young lawyer earn these kinds of bucks? Six figures right out of law school? I'm paying off all my student loans while learning more than I would anywhere else." Then sheepishly adding, "And trying my best to convince Gloria Delarosa to fall in love with me." A shrug. "Anyway, even if they don't trouble themselves to fire me this round, I'll be gone in a year or two. Maybe when the GRE case finally ends."

"*If* it finally ends."

"It will, Carney. All trains pull back into the station."

"Not the ones that go off the rails."

Another Jeremy shrug.

"O ye of little faith," he said. "You're underestimating yourself. And me. We are gonna whoop their asses."

"You think so?"

Jeremy took another shot at the basket. Swish. He turned to me and smiled. A good omen. "See?" he said.

I took a shot.

And missed.

38.

and me my clothes, boy."

My father had dropped the hospital gown he'd been wearing to the tile floor of the curtained examining cubical. I can't remember ever before seeing my old man naked. His belly was extended, his legs varicose-veined, his skin blotchy. I noticed the tremor in his hands, the deep sag of his genitals. Of course, he saw how I was looking at him. Once my eyes traveled back up to his face, I saw his glare. I don't know how else to put this. There was a mix of embarrassment and real hatred in his eyes.

He and I were in the emergency room at Mount Sinai West Hospital on Tenth Avenue. He had called me from the apartment around midnight and told me to come over and take him there.

"Mount Sinai West Hospital?" I said, still half asleep. "What's the matter? Where's Sean?"

"Get up here."

"Okay, but where's Sean?"

My father didn't answer. He hung up. I threw on some clothes and caught a cab to Hell's Kitchen.

I hadn't seen or spoken to my brother since the day of Rosy's funeral. Partly because I was wrapped up with work. But truthfully? I just didn't want to deal with his drinking and drugging.

As for my old man, he had ignored enough symptoms (blood in his urine, pissing his pants, back and abdominal pain) to cause the need for this hospital run, and after a three-hour-long battery of tests, the attending doc privately gave me what turned out to be a correct diagnosis.

"We need some more tests but I'm pretty sure your father has bladder cancer," the doc said as we stood out in the hall.

A gurney flew by accompanied by a shouting medical team trying to triage some bloodied teenager who was writhing and lurching in pain, his torso ripped apart from what looked like some sort of gun blast. The doc didn't seem to notice. For him this was far from an isolated occurrence.

"How bad? If you're right?"

"Best guess? It's most likely what we call superficial bladder cancer. Only the bladder lining will be affected, not the bladder's muscle walls. It's treatable. It won't kill him, but I know what will."

"Meaning?"

This doctor must have been about Jeremy's age, but even in the white lab coat and stethoscope snake-wrapped around his neck and the black-rimmed geek eyeglasses, he looked like someone playing the doctor in a high-school production of *Our Town*.

"Meaning your father has a fairly advanced case of cirrhosis of the liver. He doesn't stop drinking? That's what will kill him."

And that was when I walked back into the cubicle and saw my old man drop his gown to the floor.

I reached over to the small side table and took hold of his street clothes. "Want some help?" I asked.

He waved me away with a dismissive sweep of his hand. I tossed his clothes to the gurney next to where he was standing and watched my dad struggle as he twice almost keeled over from trying to guide his feet into his undershorts and slacks. Each time I started near him, he snapped at me to leave him "the fook" alone.

In the cab on the short ride back to the apartment, I asked him if he'd understood what the doctor had said to him after he was dressed.

"What does he know?" my father said, once again waving it all dismissively away. "He's just some snot-nosed kid. A doctor? Ach, my aching arse."

"It's simple, Dad," I said when he'd finished. "You keep drinking, you die."

"Well, aren't I the lucky one?" he said, purposefully turning his face from me and toward his window. It was still dark out, dawn at least a good hour away. "To be blessed with this posh, educated lad who's not only a highbrow lawyer but also miraculously schooled in the fine art of healing."

Fuck it, I told myself as my father continued staring out his window. *Let it go. Take him home. Then go home.*

I dropped him off. Walked him up to the apartment. But I didn't go home. Once back on the street, I pulled out my cell and called my brother.

Three rings in, he answered.

"Hey, Carney," he said. I could hear the sleep in his voice. "What's up, bro?"

39.

I watched my brother pour three full packets of sugar into his coffee.

He was seated across from me in a booth at a diner on Eleventh Avenue, not far from the Hell's Kitchen apartment. To give Sean credit, it didn't take him long to show up after my call. He looked like shit, though not much different really from how he'd looked ever since Iraq, just thinner and paler. He needed a shave, and his hair was longer and shaggier than last time, but not any kind of fashion statement.

"That's a lot of sugar, Sean."

And that's when he let me know that he'd gotten himself hooked on heroin, despite what had happened to Rosy.

It was still early morning, and the diner was pretty full with those making a pit stop for a hurried breakfast before embedding themselves in their offices or delivery trucks or whatever. Glass, china, and utensils were quietly clattering. There was a buzz in the place, but a fairly subdued one given the hour and the collective need for coffee. The morning was warm, and Sean was in T-shirt, jeans, and unlaced high-top sneakers. I made a grab across the table and examined my brother's arms, looking for track marks among the tattoos.

"No telltale lines, bro," he said. "I shoot up between my toes. Old trick."

Why would Sean just come out and tell me of his new addiction? That was Sean. My brother. Really as simple as that.

The waitress came by to take our order. Scrambled eggs and a toasted bagel for me. Sean smiled at the waitress, who seemed interested in him despite his road-weary look.

"Just coffee," he told her.

"Nothin' to eat?" she asked, concerned. (How women have always wanted to mother him.)

Sean pointed to his coffee mug.

"Just coffee, babe," he said with that Sean smile.

Things I didn't say to my brother once the waitress was out of earshot: *How could you do this? Think about Rosy and what happened to her. You're slowly killing yourself.*

I mean, why? Sean didn't need to hear that. Like, what, it hadn't occurred to him? What was the point? I loved my brother, as he knew, without limit. Sure, I was scared shitless that something catastrophic was about to body-slam him. But a lecture would have been down-right worthless.

Instead I filled him in on our old man. He listened, sipping at his coffee, smiling thanks to the waitress who kept topping him up. When I was done, he told me he didn't give a "rat's ass" what happened to our father.

Flashing *me* that Sean smile.

"The great Seamus Blake bites the dust," he said, adding, "Who the fuck cares?"

"And how are *you* getting by?"

A shrug. A sip of coffee. "Dunno. Working odd jobs. Some petty crime. You know."

"You're not living in the apartment?

Another *Who knows, who cares?* shrug from Sean. "Tell you the truth, Carney, I'm not 'living'"—here my brother held up air quotes—"anywhere."

W hile Sean and I were in that booth at the diner, Peter Moss had just entered the three-car garage of his Chevy Chase, Maryland, home. He got in behind the wheel of his Porsche 911 Turbo and fired up the engine. He then pressed the visor button to raise his garage door and carefully pulled out to make his way over to Western Avenue and then Rock Creek Park for the trip downtown to his office.

It had been six weeks since Josh's accident. Peter had chartered an air ambulance to bring the boy back to D.C. for inpatient rehab at a facility near their home. And as predicted, it was slow going, the ultimate outcome still uncertain.

When Peter left the house that morning, his wife was still in bed, where she would likely remain for the better part of the day. Dinner with her at home the night before had been the latest in an increasing number of tense encounters. At her end of the table, she would alternate between monastic silence and mournful laments over her fate, by which she meant *their* fate.

His prior efforts to console her had been paper thin. Even he could hear the lip service he was paying as he repeatedly told her that things would work out somehow. Patricia would then berate him.

"Work out somehow? How the hell would you know? You're hardly ever here. And when you are here, your head is somewhere else. Are you listening to me?"

Peter couldn't stand it. He was a prisoner, doing family time.

So he shut her out, like last night: Peter seated at his end of the table, retreating into the iPhone stationed at his elbow, working his way through the most recent batch of e-mails, as Patricia pushed her food around her plate, all the while throwing eye daggers at him.

"Put that away."

"Okay."

But he didn't.

"Put it away, goddamn it."

He continued reading and sending.

Peter didn't hear Patricia's chair lurch back as she rose and went to his side of the dining-room table. Didn't see her swooping hand until it was too late, as she grabbed the phone and then with all her might flung it against the wall.

Peter maneuvered his Porsche through the park, slowing and speeding with the rush-hour flow.

Could he be a better husband? Spend more time with her? Try his best to repair her broken heart?

Could he? Or would he?

He wouldn't. It just wasn't in him.

Peter's salve for life's disappointments wasn't family. No point in wishing otherwise. When home, he was nothing special, only another nobody standing in a long line going nowhere. Of course he fretted over Josh's unfortunate fate. Just as much as she did, he told himself. But what was he supposed to do? Wallow in it? Like her?

No point in overanalyzing this, he told himself. It was what it was. Work made him feel alive. Made him somebody. So be it. And that's why as Peter Moss drove downtown, he switched mental gears to GRE and Carl Smith. And as he did, he could feel tension evaporate like steam off a boiling pot.

Taking the P Street exit out of the park, he decided that now was the time to fire up the rest of his plan. Meanwhile the object of Peter Moss's destructive desire was busy dealing with his own "family issues."

Carl Smith kept a close watch on the screen of his cell phone. It was at his elbow on his desk, much as Peter Moss's cell had been at his the night before. When it finally came to life and bleeped, Carl literally flinched. That was how intensely he'd been waiting all afternoon.

His ear to the phone, he said nothing, just listened. He could hear William's sobs.

"That bitch hurt me," he told Carl.

40.

What?"

William Cunningham was in Polly Smith's Upper East Side one-bedroom.

As Carl had instructed, he'd called Polly the day before. She knew who he was; she'd seen (courtesy of Iván) the video and the stills of William seated poolside with his hands gripping Carl's buttocks for dear life, trying his best to keep his mouth wrapped around Carl's you-know-what, as our law firm's chairman jerkily ejaculated all over the place.

William told Polly that Carl had dumped him. No human being should be treated the way he was by that dreadful man, he'd said. And that got him to thinking. Polly no doubt had suffered a similar fate at Carl's hands. And so he was prepared to do whatever was needed to help Polly get her well-deserved pound of flesh from that terrible man. He was prepared to tell her things about Carl that were so explosive that this thoroughly contemptible person would buckle at his knees and give in to each and every one of her demands.

It was all bullshit, of course, but Carl figured it would do the trick. And it did.

"Can I come over and see you?" William had asked her on the call.

"By all means," Polly had said.

And so the next day, by prearrangement, William had entered Polly's building through the back entrance, having been given the security code by Polly, who had waited out in the hall on her floor to let William in from the fire stairs. William did his best to avoid any security cameras. And he had. Well, mostly he had. He missed the one over the fifth-floor stairway entrance.

All this secrecy was necessary, William had said, because what he was going to tell her was so wild, so ugly, that he needed to be sure there would be no tracing it back to him. No one must know, he'd told Polly, at least for now. Especially not your divorce lawyer. That was okay by her, and so they made it a date.

The minute William was in Polly's apartment, he changed his tune. He shoved her out of the narrow entrance area and kept shoving her until she fell back onto the sofa in her small living room. And there he stood before her, doing his best to bulge his considerable pecs and biceps as menacingly as possible. He was only marginally convincing at this, attired as he was in a lemon yellow polo shirt with spotless matching sneakers, too-tight jeans, and salon-frosted hair.

Let's stop a minute.

You know, when I later heard about all this, I thought no way. Carl Smith hatching a plan like this? This befuddled comedy of errors? That wasn't the Carl Smith I knew. But know what?

Even the smartest and most capable among us loses track of reality when he or she is deep in the throes of marital discord. Ask any divorce lawyer. They will all confirm it. You simply wouldn't believe the behavior of even the most accomplished and brainiest of people when it comes to heaping scorn on a despised spouse. When matrimony turns into acrimony, these people will exhibit all the cool and deliberate thinking of a vindictive twelve-year-old with enraged hormones.

Our Carl was no exception.

So back to William doing his best to tower over Polly.

Now, even though this was late morning, Polly was drunk. She had begun imbibing earlier and earlier each day. In fact, any earlier and Polly would need to be pouring scotch over her morning cornflakes.

Carl had done his damnedest to prepare William for this confrontation. He had made the poor guy repeatedly rehearse his lines until Carl was satisfied he could pull it off.

William was to warn Polly that if she didn't get rid of her divorce lawyer this instant and allow Carl to provide for her in the manner that Carl thought best . . . well, not only would she get absolutely nothing from him—*Nada. Rien. Nichts.*—she would also be facing some very grave personal danger. It would strike her when she least expected it. And it was not going to be pretty. So Polly had better do as she was told. Or else.

And what was our Polly's three-sheets-to-the-wind response? It was the question that threw William off his script.

"So how was it?" she'd asked him.

"What?" he had said.

"How was sex with my husband? Good? Better than good? Less than good? It's a pretty straightforward question."

This was not how this was supposed to go.

Perhaps we should cut William some slack here. He was, as we've seen, not the sharpest knife in the drawer. So what does he do? Or say?

Well, nothing, mostly. Lost for words as he was, he tried out a series of facial expressions on Polly. Squinty-eyed mean. Glaring. Silently snarling. All met by Polly's mirthfully patting the empty space beside her.

"Come sit by me," she told him.

And so he did.

Polly was having trouble focusing. She had dropped a couple of high-strength Xanaxes just before William's appearance, just in case she would need to summon the courage to remain cool and calm. And there was no way in heaven or hell that Carl in his prep sessions with William—let alone this splendidly attired young man, seated so close to Polly that their thighs were pressed together—could have known that she was at that very moment internally screening a sex fantasy. Running through Polly's alcoholic brain was an HD video of the three of them in bed together, going at it, skin on skin, bodies on bodies, in some hot preorgasmic interlude.

Polly moved her face within inches of William's. She studied his eyes, his mouth. Got even closer.

"Sweetie, I'm seeing you and me and Carl, the three of us naked in bed. Are his lips as soft as mine?" she asked poor William, not giving him the time to respond before pressing her mouth to his and forcing her tongue down his throat.

Polly's eyes were slammed shut as she kept kissing William, pushing her body even closer, ensuring that her surgically enhanced breasts made a hard landing onto his bulging chest.

William, on the other hand, sat ramrod straight, his eyes large open saucers staring with understandable panic as Polly kept tonguing and embracing. His arms were lifted in what could have been seen as an impending embrace of his own to this cloyingly perfumed and boozy older woman. In reality they were simply raised in total dismay as Polly's hand slowly slid down to his crotch.

Tight jeans or no tight jeans, once Polly's hand had made contact, she had no trouble detecting that William's penis was as soft as a three-day-old peeled banana. She gave it a little squeeze. Then something snapped in her, and that gentle caress turned into a crunching, viselike grip.

"Ow! What are you doing? Stop that!"

William tried his best to disengage, but Polly's hold on his flaccid pecker only tightened. Xanax or no Xanax, Polly came to her senses and was enraged. The booze cursing through her veins provided all the necessary fuel she needed.

"You think you can come here, to my place? And scare me? You can tell that son of a bitch husband of mine he can't scare me."

"Ow! Let go of me. Please!"

Polly gave William one more seismic penis crunch and then released her hand. But before William could move away, she slapped him hard across his face. Polly was enflamed, any theoretical rationality by then much too far gone for retrieval.

She sprang to her feet, and now it was she who was towering over William. Pointing an accusing finger at him.

"You pathetic pansy. Waltzing in here thinking you can scare me."

"You hurt me," William whimpered, still in the throes of severe penis pain. "You shouldn't have done that."

"Really!" Polly screamed back at him. "I hurt your poor little flaccid dick? Well, I'll tell you what—you can inform Carl that if he sends you back here again, I'll cut off your teensy winky and FedEx it to him. You both disgust me."

Still rubbing his crotch, William stayed where he was. That is, until Polly leaned over and spit right in his face. That did it.

He got to his feet.

"How dare you!" he yelled at her as he wiped her spit off his face with the back of his hand and then grabbed her hard by the neck.

"Go ahead, try it," Polly said to him, glaring, her eyes on fire. "You don't have the balls."

So William accepted Polly's brash invitation and started squeezing. Harder and harder. In no time at all, Polly's panicked eyes started bulging, she began gurgling, and then her face and lips started turning blue. Another few seconds and Polly would be a goner. But in the nick of time, he let go.

Polly fell to her knees choking, her own hands now reflexively at her neck. William watched for a while as she gasped for air. Then he grabbed her by an arm and flung her back onto the sofa, where she sat gasping and coughing.

William stormed from the apartment, making it out to the street by the same back-way path through which he had entered Polly's building. (And once again tripping the fifth-floor security camera.) Out on the sidewalk, he made that call to Carl.

When the police eventually found Polly a few days later, lying faceup on her bed, stone-cold dead, they figured her a suicide.

After William's hasty exit, Polly must have spent some time on the sofa trying to compose herself. As best the cops could figure, at some point she probably got up and went to her bathroom, where she removed the Xanax vial from her medicine cabinet and took a few more pills. That extra dosage, combined with the lethal amount of scotch she'd earlier ingested, had put her out like the proverbial light. The prescription bottle was found on her night table, where she had placed it before lying down, faceup, on the bed.

Unfortunately for Polly she was too deeply asleep when, some-time in the middle of the night, the cops concluded, she began vom-iting and swallowing so much of what she was chucking up that she choked to death on her own puke.

At least that was the medical examiner's initial finding. There were traces of vomit around her mouth, and her lungs weighed in heavier than normal, given the upchuck she'd swallowed.

Ah, but.

Both the police and the coroner had detected bruising around Polly's neck. Evidence, needless to say, of foul play. What's more, they were miraculously able to lift some partial fingerprints belong-ing to our young gym rat off Polly's cold neck flesh (medical science does advance), as well as finding enough of William's DNA in the living room of her apartment to clone him several times over. And then there were the freeze frames from the fifth-floor security camera showing William going up the back stairwell, then soon thereafter hurriedly leaving the same way.

An investigation was begun, though, for the time being, death by suicide remained the (provisional) finding.

Was Carl worried?

Probably.

He carefully studied the autopsy report. So if it came to it, he had a backup plan. This one also involved William.

Though not in a way William was going to like.

41.

olly Smith's obituary made the *New York Times*.

She was featured just below the obit of a twenty-something rock-star drummer who had piloted his private plane (and its three female passengers) into the side of a mountain. His autopsy revealed enough dope in his veins to fuel at least ten rows of fans that had attended the stadium concert the evening before his fatal flight.

Like the rocker's, Polly's obit featured an accompanying photo. It clearly looked to be from times past, with a delighted Polly in sundress with her hand securing a floppy hat as she leaned against a stiff breeze at the rail of someone's yacht. The *Times* did not provide a cause of death. Carl got next-of-kin billing, noting that he was "chairman of one of America's most prominent law firms." Their decade-long-AWOL daughter (who neither showed up for the funeral nor sent a card, electronic or paper) was also named.

As next of kin, Carl was required under New York law to identify Polly's body at the medical examiner's office. He did, telling the ME that his poor, lamentable wife had been severely depressed ever since their estrangement. Shaking his head with the utter sadness of it all, he also made sure to mention Polly's out-of-control drinking. (Nothing was said to him at the time about the marks found on her neck. As I said, he would later catch that in the autopsy report.)

"So very tragic," Carl just about whispered, shaking his head in post-connubial grief, while managing to squeeze out a tear or two.

A terse e-mail about Polly's untimely death was circulated throughout Dunn & Sullivan. It was left at that. *Coffee break's over, back to work.* Carl stayed away from his office for only a day or two. Once back, he acknowledged hallway expressions of sympathy wordlessly, with a slightly altered version of the Carl Smith head nod. There was, however, one task Carl saw to during his "mourning" period.

He paid a visit to the law offices of Iván the Impaler.

Polly's divorce case had died with her. So the prospect of a continuing handsome legal fee for lawyer Escobar was no longer to be. But there was still the matter of those pesky photos and the accompanying video. A loose end that needed tidying up, so to speak.

Iván was later questioned under oath about his meeting with Carl.

> **Lawyer:** How long after Polly Smith's death did her husband pay his visit to you?
> **Iván:** The day after.
> **Lawyer:** What did he want?
> **Iván:** Why don't you ask him?
> **Lawyer:** I'm asking you.

On the deposition video, you can see Iván smirk. He fingers his perfectly situated necktie. He's letting the questioner—a junior lawyer with a timid voice—know: *Don't even think about fucking with me.* He's also testing this kid, seeing how easily he can be pushed.

> **Iván:** I'm not sure what he wanted. All I can tell you is what he said.

Lawyer: (*The young lawyer ignores Iván's baited-hook comment and doesn't then ask, "So what did he say?" That would have given Iván room to assert some open-ended, self-serving bullshit about his claim of what Carl had said. Instead, to pin Carl down, the lawyer asks . . .*) Carl Smith wanted something from you, didn't he?

Iván: Did he?

Lawyer: Yes, in fact he did. He wanted the return of certain . . . let's call them troublesome photos and an accompanying video. You remember that, don't you?

Iván: Yes.

Lawyer: Smith bought them from you, didn't he?

Iván: No.

Lawyer: Well, let's talk about that.

Iván: That's not a question. You need to ask me a question.

Lawyer: Smith told you he was there to see you as next of kin and as executor of his deceased wife's estate. And not as the counterparty to the terminated divorce proceeding. You remember that, don't you?

Iván: (*Nods his head yes.*)

Lawyer: You will need to answer verbally, Mr. Escobar. You're a lawyer. You know that. (*This young lawyer clearly doesn't like this overdressed, smug divorce lawyer. Good for him.*)

Iván: Yes.

Lawyer: And Smith asked you, as executor, to hand over his deceased wife's entire file, all papers and all exhibits. You remember that, too, don't you?

Iván: Yes.

Lawyer: And you complied with Smith's request, didn't you?

Iván: Yes.

Lawyer: And he paid you for that effort, didn't he?

Iván: I think he did.

Lawyer: What was your hourly rate at the time?

Iván: Eight hundred dollars an hour.

Lawyer: And it took you . . . what? Ten minutes to comply with Smith's request? Go to your file cabinet. Pull out the file—all the papers and exhibits, including the photos and the video. Then pass it across your desk to Carl Smith?

Iván: About that.

Lawyer: And can you recall how much you charged him for this ten-minute effort?

Iván: No, I can't.

The lawyer pulls a document from a file lying on the table beside him. He asks the stenographer to mark the document as Exhibit One. After the stenographer does that . . .

Lawyer: (*sliding the document across the table to Iván*) Mr. Escobar. Please take a look at what has been marked as deposition Exhibit One and tell me if you can identify that document.

Iván: It appears to be a photocopy of a canceled check.

Lawyer: Appears to be?

Iván: It is.

Lawyer: And to whom is the check made out?

Iván: To me.

Lawyer: And who signed it?

Iván: Carl Smith.

Lawyer: And how much is it made out for?

Iván: A hundred thousand dollars.

Lawyer: And so Carl Smith paid you one hundred thousand dollars for your ten minutes of work, consisting of your turning over to him a file, a batch of photos, and an accompanying video. Right?

Iván: I think I would like to consult with counsel before I answer
that question.

Thereupon the deposition was suspended for the day.

I had seen the firmwide e-mail about Polly's death, but I didn't give
it much thought at the time. My mind was elsewhere.

Peter Moss had sent me a notice scheduling my deposition. That
notice was like a loaded gun to my head.

You see, unlike the main case where I was acting as a lawyer and
so essentially exempt from interrogation, in the stand-alone case
Moss had brought, I was a party defendant and not counsel of record.
So I could be compelled to sit for a deposition like any other witness.
Put under oath and questioned. And since both cases dealt with the
same general set of facts, by interrogating me in case number two
Moss would make me a witness against myself in case number one.

He was playing chess with me. Scheduling my deposition in the
second case was his latest move.

Moss was not about to restrict his questioning. He'd grill me about
everything, whether it was legally privileged or not. Was there any
way I could stop him?

Not likely. Of course, I could have taken the Fifth and refused to
answer questions on self-incrimination grounds. But no fucking way
was I about to do that. For two reasons: One, I hadn't done anything
wrong. Two, I took the Fifth? How was I going to explain *that* to the bar?

I had been placed in check. Was it checkmate?

No.

The deposition never went forward.

Why?

It starts with Jeremy Lichtman.

42.

eremy walked into my office.

Just as he shut the door, I once again caught sight of Richard Miller racing down the hallway.

"We need to talk," Jeremy said as he took the chair facing me.

I was still consumed with my deposition dilemma and was about to ask him what he thought I should do, but the look on Jeremy's usually tranquil face stopped me. He was clearly agitated.

"What's up?" I asked.

"This," he said as he pulled out his smartphone and pushed SEND. I heard the whoosh of his message and the almost immediate ping on my laptop screen.

"Take a look."

Jeremy had sent me an attachment that contained an Excel spreadsheet, something he'd apparently created. I opened it, lowered my eyes, and started reading.

"How'd you get this information?" I asked midway through the document.

"The first part I just ran a search of our law firm's client files." Anticipating my next question—*why* he'd gotten the information—he quickly added, "Tell you the truth, I wasn't sure what I was looking for. Call it instinct, whatever. I don't know, something just told me that this GRE case was weird enough I should take a look around. See what else the firm recently brought in."

What Jeremy had found and then indexed was a listing of five new class-action plaintiffs' cases, including our GRE case. All were on contingent fees. All had been assigned to relatively new Dunn & Sullivan litigation partners. All had been financed by hedge funds. And all were listed as under the supervision of Carl Smith.

I looked up.

"Check out the total amount of damages claimed."

I ran my eyes back down the spreadsheet and saw the totaling of all the cases. The amount was in the billions. The firm's contingent-fee interest in each case was also totaled. An eye-popping number.

"So," I said. "The firm is changing its new case-intake policies. Strange for a firm like ours, but still . . ."

"Keep reading," Jeremy said, cutting me off in midsentence.

I did.

Jeremy had somehow hacked into Carl Smith's personal files. Attached to the spreadsheet were excerpts from Carl's electronic diary and an assortment of e-mails, notes, and a draft stock-transfer pledge. The name of the recipient was still blank.

"What the fuck?" I asked Jeremy. "What did you do?"

"Paid a late-night visit to Carl's secretary's computer terminal. Wasn't hard. Looked under her desk blotter. There was Smith's password. Logged in. Easy as pie."

Searching a law firm's database for new cases was one thing. There was nothing technically wrong with that. Hacking into another lawyer's personal files, let alone the firm chairman's?

Everything was wrong with that.

"Are you out of your fucking mind? There'll be a record of your entry into Smith's computer."

"Yes, that's true. If anyone looks for it."

Jeremy removed his eyeglasses and started polishing his lenses with his necktie. He looked up. I could see fatigue rings under his eyes. He stared at me with a burning intensity. Something I hadn't seen before. This was more than some young associate sitting across from me. A lot more.

"You want to report me, fine," he added. "But first take a look at what I found."

So I did.

It wasn't hard to put the pieces together. Jeremy clearly had.

These new mega-contingent-fee cases? The young and inexperienced supervising partners? The hedge-fund financing? Carl the intake source? A clear pattern.

Were they all illegitimate cases? Maybe yes. Maybe no. But pairing even some of those new cases with Carl's other actions? There it was.

His meetings with bankers. His e-mails to them about how flush with money the firm was. His IPO efforts to be the first major law firm to go public, turning Dunn & Sullivan into a potential gold mine for whoever held large blocks of its stock on sale to the investing public. This was too clandestine. Carl was up to something. And what about that draft stock-transfer pledge? What was that all about?

"So now what?" I asked Jeremy. "Confront Smith?"

"Are you kidding?"

He was right. The chances of Carl fessing up to a newly minted partner and his midlevel associate hovered somewhere between zero and none. Okay, then what? Do nothing? That didn't work either.

We had seen too much. If Carl was somehow intent on creating a false picture of the firm's profitability to the bank's underwriters and it eventually came out, we would be justifiably faulted for not having done something to bring all this to light. It was our duty to come forward with it.

"So?" Jeremy asked.

He had figured out our next step.

"See the rabbi?" I said.

"Yeah."

I needed to go see Anka Stankowski.

Now.

43.

I was in Anka's office, laying it all out.

Had I become the Wile E. Coyote of Big Law as the Road Runner (played alternatively by Peter Moss and Carl Smith) stands at the top of a hill and pushes a huge boulder down on me? I look up at this speeding mass of granite hurtling its way to earth, and me, and then look right into the camera and murmur "Uh-oh."

I told Anka everything that Jeremy (without naming him) had found and what I thought it meant. She asked me if I had extracted all this troublesome information myself. I told her no, someone else had done it.

"Who, Carney? Who hacked into our system? That's some serious shit, to do that. Who?"

"I can't tell you."

"I'm not *asking* you to tell me, I'm *telling* you to tell me."

Despite my assurances to Jeremy, I was tempted to tell her. I wanted and needed her help, her advice, her guidance. Let's not lose sight of the fact that Anka was a powerful senior partner at Dunn & Sullivan. She was a voice that would be heard. So as Anka sat there looking at me, waiting for me to cough up the name of the hacker, I was thinking maybe I should. I mean, how could I enlist her help and at the same time hold back on her?

Just as I was about to speak, we both heard this loud noise. A bang. No, more of a sonic crack. Coming from right down the hall. It made us both flinch. We shot to our feet. (Well, someone Anka's size doesn't "shoot" to her feet, but she was up out of the chair pretty damn quickly.) We both went into the hall. The sharp smell of a fired gun was in the air. And it appeared to be coming from the corner office a few doors down from Anka's.

That was Carl Smith's office.

Anka and I and some of the others raced down there. His door was shut. His secretary was standing with her hand on the knob, frozen in place. Anka shoved her aside and opened the door with me right in behind her.

Carl was seated behind his desk. Immobile. That was the first thing we saw. Then we saw the body.

Holy shit.

Richard Miller was lying faceup on the floor in front of Carl's desk. His arms were outstretched Jesus-like, that massive chest of his completely still. The left side of his face was missing. Gobs of blood and bone fragments were puddling around his open wound. (Behind me I heard someone retch.) That goo seeping out of Miller was thick and sticky-looking and coppery-smelling, and it was saturating Carl's priceless Persian rug. In Mad Dog's extended hand was a pistol.

"Carl? Are you okay?" Anka asked, carefully stepping closer toward him.

Nothing from him. He just sat there. Anka looked down.

Carl had wet his pants.

"It's all over Twitter."

"I know," I told Diane. "But the real details aren't out yet."

The evening after Miller's death, Diane and I were having dinner together. The date had been arranged the previous week. I was the one who had called. We were in my neighborhood on the Upper West Side at Bar Boulud, on Broadway and West Sixty-fourth Street across from Lincoln Center.

Diane at first didn't show. I sat at our table in this long, skinny restaurant with its blond wooden decor, wondering and then worrying that she wasn't going to come. But she did.

I saw her charge into the restaurant and then wait impatiently in line for the maître d's attention before spotting me and quickly coming over.

"Sorry," she'd said as she hurriedly took the seat opposite mine (no kiss, no hug), "but the judge held counsel over after the jury was excused for the day. Seems he wanted to share his displeasure with both sides for whatever. You know the drill," she added, shrugging.

I was so happy to see her. I was just kind of nodding, sure, okay, no problem. She looked great. It was technically spring, but the New York weather was very much summer. Diane was still in her going-to-court outfit, this one noticeably lightweight, though with courtroom-appropriate dark coloring. Her hair was schoolmarm up, and those eyes were lovely as ever. The top few buttons of her white blouse were unfastened, something I was certain she'd taken care of after she left the downtown courthouse to subway it up to the West Side.

I was nursing a vodka martini. Diane eyeballed it and then caught the waiter's attention, wordlessly signaling, *One of those, too, please.* In no time the waiter slid her drink in front of her.

That was when she told me that Mad Dog's death was all over Twitter.

Electronic news has its obvious advantages—you learn everything within seconds of its happening. But only headlines. For real detail you need to wait. You could try cable-TV news, but all they do is talk the headlines to death.

The police had spent the rest of the day at Dunn & Sullivan taking statements and doing forensics. By the time the medical examiner's office had bagged Mad Dog's remains and gurneyed him down the service elevator to street level and the waiting meat wagon, we at the firm at least were able to piece the story together.

"You want to hear the gory details?" I asked Diane as she sipped her martini.

"Are you kidding? Of course."

So I told her.

It begins with Miller racing down the hall (past my office, as I've said). For the past few weeks, Mad Dog had been exhibiting more of his rage and bombast than usual. Carl had succeeded in isolating Richard to the degree that he had no place to turn. We later learned that he had tried to move to another law firm, but no one would have him. His reputation, I guess, preceded him. And then he snapped.

He barged his way into Carl's office, furiously kicking the door shut behind him. He took up a position at the foot of Carl's desk, enraged. Carl said nothing, waiting him out. Miller glaring, murderous. Carl told the cops the standoff had lasted for a while, neither man speaking.

Then Carl instructed Miller to go back to his office.

"My office?" Richard screamed. "My office? For what? To sit there and stare into space? You've ruined my practice! My life! And now, you goddamn son of a bitch, it's time to pay!"

"Richard—" was as far as Carl got when he saw the gun in Miller's hand.

"That's right," Miller said as he followed Carl's eyes down to the gun he was holding. "That's right, you . . . you. You fucking, you . . ."

At that point Miller was pretty much beyond words. He didn't finish his sentence. Instead he raised the gun and aimed it dead level at Carl's head.

Carl didn't move, eyeing the gun, as he told the police, convinced that Richard was going to kill him right then and there. (Carl glossed over his urinary mishap, though the cops later joked about the wet spot they saw on this fancy lawyer's fancy pants.)

Miller was rabid. Carl told the police that the guy was actually growling.

And then he pulled the trigger.

Nothing. A click. Only a click. He fired a second time. Another click. Carl didn't move a muscle. Miller pulled the trigger a third time. A third click.

Carl watched Richard, perplexed, raise the pistol off his target, trying to figure what the problem was. Carl told the police he started thinking, did Miller have an empty gun? Had he forgotten to load it?

Paralyzed by fear as he was, Carl stared straight ahead as Richard studied the gun, now angled up toward himself (Richard was no marksman and most likely hadn't ever actually fired a gun before.) He must have looked like some kid trying to figure out how to operate a complex new toy. And of course that's when the gun actually went off, its blast shearing off the left side of Richard Miller's head.

The explosion was deafening in the relatively small confines of Carl's office. Carl watched, temporarily deaf, ears ringing, as Richard's flesh and bone splattered on the back wall. Miller remained standing, now with only one eye still intact. His eyeglasses had been blown away, but he seemed to be staring at Carl, the expression on his face (Carl told the police) inquisitive. *What the hell was that?* he seemed to be thinking. Well, Richard Miller probably wasn't thinking anything. He was dead on his feet (is that where the expression comes from?) and just didn't know it yet.

Then Miller let out this massive sigh, sort of a *Can you beat that?* And then fell backward onto Carl's Persian carpet in the position Anka and I found him in when she barged into Carl's office with me right behind her.

So maybe Richard Miller was Wile E. Coyote.

By the time I finished the story, Diane and I were midway through our meals (we had ordered somewhere around Miller's barging into Carl's office). It felt so good being with her. We ate in silence for a while, each from time to time glancing at the other. My apartment was only a ten-minute walk from here. I was tempted, but I said nothing about our maybe, you know, going over there to raid my freezer for ice cream. Not that I had any.

And then our meals over, the dishes taken away, dessert and coffee declined, Diane swirling the last bit of wine left in her glass. Studying me.

God, she was beautiful. I looked back into those green eyes that were swallowing me whole.

The waiter dropped the check off at our table. It was late, too late for our table to turn over. So I got the impression that he didn't care if we lingered.

And that's what we did. In fact, we were the last patrons to leave the place.

We sat and talked. About a lot of things. Personal things.

Including, for once, race.

I talked about my father's rancid bigotry. How I'd let it go. Gave him a pass. Telling her, what was the point? No way was I going to change him. But what about me? What was I doing with a black woman? Was that really a nonissue? Or was there some kind of illusory rebellion I was after?

"You're a white guy, Carney. From Hell's Kitchen. Under the circumstances I'd say you're doing just fine." Here she paused. Thinking what?

"Tell me?" I said.

She finished off the inch of wine remaining in her glass. Then looked at me some more before responding.

"I keep asking myself, is my attraction to you because you are white? No, I keep thinking. That's not me," she said. "But am I kidding myself? Subconsciously stepping up? Do I want into your world and simply won't own up to it? A white lover? A Big Law life?"

I had to chuckle. *My world? Who in her right mind would want into my world?*

"Careful what you ask for. You've seen me at my worst. My advice? Give my world the kind of pass I give my old man."

Like I said, we sat there at that table for a good long while. Patching things up. Talking. Really talking.

I've thought about that evening many times. Diane was the one lucky break I'd gotten. We were opposites in many ways. Color being just one of them. She cared for me. And I for her. I knew I needed to do whatever I could to hang on to that. Screw the rest.

We didn't hold hands across the table. Nothing lovey-dovey going on. At least overtly. Just us. Being us.

Then breaking the spell.

"Sean?" Diane asked. "How's he doing?"

I told her about my breakfast with my brother and how he'd looked, what he'd said.

"I don't know, Diane," I said. "I hope he's okay. That he can come to terms with his addiction. There's a lot to Sean. If he can catch a break or two for once in his life, I know he can get himself through this."

Diane kept looking at me, shaking her head. "I hope he does, Carney," she said. "I really hope he does."

He didn't.

44.

It turned into a twofer day.

I got both calls very early the next morning, when the guards allow inmates phone privileges. The first call came at 6:00 a.m., the second less than an hour later.

The first call:

A very sleepy "Hello" from me after I managed to grab my cell off the floor by my bed after knocking it off the night table while groping for it somewhere between the fourth and fifth rings. Diane rolled over and groaned. (So we wound up at my place that night after all.)

"Counselor," the voice said. A voice I couldn't place but knew I knew. "Time to pay your bill."

My response?

A repeat "Hello?"

"Wake up, motherfucker. And get your fancy ass down here. I want bail, and I want it now."

Oh, shit. Him. The guy from the 112th Street apartment. The Hispanic drug dealer. Since our last meeting, I'd learned his name. Geraldo. Garaldo? Something or other.

"Where are you?"

"Where am I? I'm sitting at the bar at the Four Seasons Hotel sipping a motherfucking piña colada."

Still half asleep. "What?"

Now actually screaming at me. "I'm at the Metropolitan Correctional Center! I go before the judge later today. You owe me, motherfucker. Remember? You don't step up? All bets are off. You can kiss your junkie brother good-bye." Then, after apparently being admonished by a guard to keep his voice down. To the guard, "Okay, okay. No problem. Aright?" Then back to me, "You comin' or what?"

"I'll be there soon as I can."

"Get here fucking sooner," he said, no longer screaming because the guard was no doubt keeping a watchful eye on him as he stood by the wall of inmate phones. Then he hung up.

Just what I needed, I was thinking as I slipped out of bed, hurriedly showered and shaved. I was speed-eating a bowl of Rice Chex and mainlining coffee, Diane in the shower, when the second call came in.

Here's that call:

At first I thought it was him calling back, with that same prison-inmate noise in the background.

Then, from the other end of the line, "Bro?"

I could hear a bunch of angry men shouting, hurling insults, just making a general racket. *Oh, no,* I started thinking. *Him, too? On the same day?*

Yup, him too.

"Sean?"

"Guess I need some help, bro," he said above that awful racket. I could picture my brother standing by the bank of phones by the wall (just like my earlier caller), one finger in his ear so he could hear me.

"Where?"

"Manhattan Central Booking, 100 Centre Street."

Manhattan Correctional Center, where the drug dealer was being held, was for federal prisoners. Manhattan Central Booking was a different jail, one for state prisoners. So at least these two weren't in the same jail. A blessing? That would be overstating it. Better than horrible? I'll go with that.

"Be there as soon as I can," I told Sean, leaving out that I had another stop to make first.

"Okay, bro. I'm good. Get here when you can."

I was about to hang up. I hadn't asked what he was being held on. Murder? What if he'd killed someone? Oh, Christ.

"What are they charging you with?"

"Criminal trespass and burglary."

"Use of a weapon?"

"Unclear."

"Okay, okay, I'll be there soon as I can," I told him, somewhat relieved.

"Thanks, bro," Sean said, and hung up.

I was halfway to the subway when I realized I hadn't said goodbye to Diane. I tried her cell. She didn't pick up, so I left her a hurried voice mail as I jostled my way down the crowded station steps.

45.

No time to go to my office. Too much to do.

By 3:00 p.m. I was seated in the courtroom used by one of the magistrates in the federal district court at 500 Pearl Street in downtown Manhattan. I had spent the morning first at one jail and then the other. (I'll get to that.)

The afternoon session scheduled in this courtroom was about to begin. Magistrates—or magistrate judges, as they're called—are the workhorses (beasts of burden?) of the federal court system. They're sort of junior judges. Federal judges exist through the U.S. Constitution, are appointed by the president with the approval of the Senate, and have the job for life. Federal magistrates are appointed for eight-year terms by the judges of the court in which they sit. The magistrates are the courtroom domestics who sweep up the dirty work of the day's docket. Their job is to tend to routine matters, in theory to free up the judges for more important . . . well, judging.

This courtroom was packed with the criminal bar. Squeezed shoulder to shoulder on the courtroom's dark wooden benches sat a fashion array running from ill-fitting off-the-rack suits and lunch-stained neckties to the flamboyantly overdressed style favored by

Iván the Impaler. Everyone (including, today, me) waiting for the magistrate to hear his or her clients' cases. Pleas would be entered (almost always "Not guilty"). Bail would be set or denied.

Judging by the babel of conversation, including the occasional argument, this was far from a refined lot. Not, however, to be confused with a dull lot. Some of the sharpest legal minds populated this world. And these lawyers knew the courtroom inside out. It's where they lived. Their law offices? Essentially unnecessary. A place for mail drops and late-afternoon sofa naps.

The guy next to me had just finished reading his copy of the *New York Times*. He nudged me.

"Want it?" he said.

There were a few fingerprint stains on the paper from the Starbursts he'd been nibbling as he repeatedly licked his thumb to turn the pages. Nothing too bad, kind of what you might see when you pick up a discarded newspaper off the subway bench. Okay, some of you wouldn't pick it up. Fine.

"Thanks," I said as I accepted his offer, doing my best to avoid touching the dark crimson bits in the margins.

Just as I opened the paper, I heard the bailiff shout for all to rise, that the court was now back in session, the Honorable Anthony Fazzano, magistrate judge for the Southern District of New York, presiding. I rose with everyone else and remained on my feet until the magistrate motioned us all back down onto our benches.

The bailiff (an out-of-central-casting heavyset, jowly guy in a suit I think he slept in) called the first case. The side door not far from the judge's bench opened, and a federal marshal in blue blazer and gray slacks led out the first shackled and jumpsuited inmate. He stationed his shuffling prisoner at the defendant's table and stepped in close behind, just in case his continued services might be needed should the guy get any ideas.

And that was the pattern. Case after case. The charges read, the magistrate asking, "How do you plead, guilty or not guilty?" The defense lawyers making bail arguments. Bail either set or not. The shackled defendant hauled away. The next orange-clad defendant(s) frog-marched in. This was the judicial version of wham, bam, thank you, ma'am.

As I said, earlier that morning I had been to the two jails.

By the time I got to the federal facility at 150 Park Row (before 9:00 a.m.), there was already a line of people waiting to visit inmates. They were patiently standing there, more or less single file, mostly black and Hispanic, mostly women and children. An unhappy bunch. They looked so horribly downtrodden. Really an upsetting sight.

There was a separate queue for the lawyers. The lawyers got priority. It didn't take long at all for me to gain entry to the building, then pass through the metal detector and go to a designated interview room. All the while that other line of impoverished and tragic-looking friends and family moved at a snail's pace, the guards shouting repeated word-for-word instructions as though these people were a bunch of abject morons. No one voiced a complaint. "Trouble-makers" were most likely sent to the back of the line.

My client, Geraldo, was led into the interview room in chains. The jailers just about shoved him into the chair facing me at the small metal desk where I was seated. The desk was bolted to the cement floor. The dealer's leg shackles were fastened to an iron loop in the floor, and his wrist shackles were attached to another loop on the top of the table. He was kind of beat-up-looking, sporting a black eye and some nasty abrasions on his face and arms. Had that happened at the arrest or in the jail?

"You want us to stay in here with you, Counselor."

This jailer was rat-faced. Not white, but who knows what? In his starched uniform, half military-, half police-looking. Hollow-cheeked. Short-cropped kinky hair. Pinprick eyes. Quite a comparison with his

Barney Fife clone of a string-bean sidekick, standing timidly near the door, clearly ready to bolt at the first sign of trouble.

"No, I don't."

"Up to you."

I watched him shrug at the other guard like I had just made the mistake of my life. Then they left. I almost jumped out of my seat when the steel door behind me slammed shut and the bolt clanged into place.

Alone now. Geraldo staring at me across the table. Waiting. Visibly angry. Where to start? I watched him shift in his seat, causing some disconcerting chain rattling.

I cleared my throat. "How you doing?"

"What?" he barked.

The guy's in federal custody, shackled to the cement floor, charged with conspiracy drug dealing, and felony murders. Yes, murders, as in multiple. Facing life in prison, no parole. And *How you doing?* I ask him.

Bad icebreaker, I admit.

I quickly removed his indictment from my briefcase and laid it on the table.

"Let's start here," I said, and we then managed to get down to business.

What I learned from him was that his entire operation and virtually all of his crew had been taken down in this massive drug bust. The FBI, the DEA, and several New York State law-enforcement joint task-force divisions were all involved. The case had been made through wiretaps. There were hours upon hours of recorded talks, many of them incriminating conversations between Geraldo and his lieutenants.

"Some of my boys were picked up by the state guys," he told me.

His point?

"Your point?" I asked.

"You think you're the only one who knows that your brother got popped and's sitting down the street, like me here? My boys in there keeping tabs on the motherfucker, know what I'm sayin'?"

I did.

If I didn't perform for Geraldo, like get him bail . . . well, Sean would be the one to pay for that.

"Look," I told him, "you need to get an experienced criminal lawyer. Let me find you someone—"

"No dice, motherfucker," he said, cutting me off as he bent his head within wrist-shackle range and touched his forefinger to his nose. "My . . . how do you say it? My intuition says you. So you better fucking get me bail today. You do? I'm gone, man. History. We clear on this, Counselor?"

"Clear."

"Yeah," he continued, rattling his wrist chains for emphasis. "Out of this motherfucking miserable country, someplace nobody's gonna find me."

Miserable country?

This didn't seem like the best time to give this scumbag, my new client, a civics lesson. So I just nodded, *Okay, got that.* And besides, guys like him probably never went anywhere. They stayed in their neighborhoods, where their action was. Where they were kings.

An hour later I was at 100 Centre Street, standing on one side of a set of bars, Sean on the other, in a large holding cell that must have had thirty men in it. Interview rooms in the state system?

Forget about it.

46.

I leaned in close to the bars.

Sean laid out what had happened: A car-repair shop in Astoria, Queens. A late-night break-in, Sean and two other junkies looking for the cashbox, or maybe some tools to steal and fence.

The owner had endured one break-in too many and so had taken to sleeping nights in his cubbyhole of an office on some ratty Barcalounger. He hears the clumsy B&E, and in two seconds flat he's got all three of them down on the floor, holding a shotgun at their heads as he cradles his phone in the crook of his neck 911-ing them. One of the guys (not Sean) had a starter's pistol stuffed in his tighty-whiteys.

As Sean was telling me all this, another inmate in the holding tank, an absolute behemoth, staggered over. This guy, African (as I judged by his accent), six foot eight at least, with heavily tattooed tree-trunk arms growing out of a sleeveless T-shirt, put one of those massive limbs around Sean's shoulders.

"Look here," he said. (Sounded like "Luke he-a.")

Sean and I stopped and gazed up at this giant. He leaned in to the bars, closer to me.

"You a lawyer?" ("Loyaaa?")

Here we go, I started thinking. *Here we go.*

I watched as Sean started patting the big guy's shoulder like he was some frisky Great Dane pup. The guy didn't budge, standing there with his arm still in place around Sean's neck.

"Cool down, big guy," Sean said.

I could see this guy's eyes were kaleidoscopes. Whatever he was on, it was powerful.

"I want you to be my loyaaa, too," the guy told me.

Sean kept gently patting the guy's shoulder, also nodding, *Yeah, sure, okay, gotcha.*

"Yo," Sean then told the guy, "this is my brother. Family. Understand? He's not no lawyer."

The jolly black giant started nodding appreciatively. Sure, family. Equating that with the apparent need for some privacy over here.

"Okayyy," he said, his freaky bloodshot eyes still captivating me. "I wheel geeve you and your brodda some privacy." (Which he pronounced in the Queen's English, "PRIV-uh-see.")

I watched as he stumbled back to the bench attached to the holding cell's far wall. He roughly pushed aside some long-haired, skinny white kid sitting where he wanted to be and took a seat. Then he smiled over at me. I gave him a little thank-you wave.

Sean looked at me. Just shrugged. It was what it was.

My brother's arraignment was scheduled in the state court's morning session, so I got to handle that before hightailing it over to the nearby federal courthouse for Geraldo. When Sean's case was called, I told the judge all about his impressive war record and his PTSD (posttraumatic stress disorder).

The judge released Sean on his own recognizance, meaning he didn't need to put up any bail, just promise on threat of further charges to show up in court when required. The judge also suggested I look into a deferred-prosecution arrangement with the DA so Sean wouldn't have a record when all this was over for him. And also rehab for his addiction.

And then I hoofed it to the federal court for its afternoon session, where I was sitting thumbing through the *Times*, waiting for my case to be called.

On the front page of the local section was the story of Miller's death. The paper got it mostly right. Below the article was a little teaser suggesting that the reader might also want to see the story appearing on the front page of the day's business section about Dunn & Sullivan and its "brain-drain loss," as the notice put it. I turned to that section and started reading.

What the fuck?

The story, another in the paper's continuing coverage of the travails of Big Law, was about the loss of my law firm's entire Washington, D.C., office. A total defection. To? Yup. Mason Rose. Peter Moss was quoted as saying that Dunn & Sullivan's glory days were over. He also talked about his suit against Dunn & Sullivan in the GRE case, mentioning me by name. (The reporter had never contacted me for comment. Wasn't he supposed to?)

Moss called me a young partner who had lost his ethical way and now stood accused of professional misconduct. I read on, my jaw dropping. Moss said that I was a criminal, that to his "shock and amazement" I kept pursuing a case where perjury and bribery (of the Indian judge) had taken place. I had just gotten to the part about "sources" saying that a grand-jury investigation of my (allegedly criminal) behavior had been empaneled when the bailiff called my case.

I didn't hear it. Astonished. Stupefied. Reading and rereading that sentence about me. Then the lawyer who had handed me the *Times* nudged me.

"That you?" he said.

Me? What?

The bailiff: "Last call. Is counsel for the defendant Geraldo Alvarez in the courtroom?"

I shook my head free of cobwebs and rose.

"Yes!" I shouted, way too loud. "Yes, I'm here," I said.

As I grabbed my file and raced to the front of the courtroom, I saw my client standing facing me.

Staring daggers.

47.

ounsel, are you sure you're in the right place?"

"Excuse me?"

"I said, 'Counsel, are you sure you're in the right place?'" the magistrate reiterated.

I was standing at the defendant's trial table. Geraldo (still chained, cuffed, and jumpsuited) stood by my side all the while, warning me under his breath that I had better fucking get him bail or else.

I was here, of course, after having raced up to the well of the court when finally realizing that my case had been (repeatedly) called. As I stood facing the magistrate, my brain was flooded by riptide thoughts of an incoming grand-jury tsunami heading straight for me.

And this junior judge was asking me if I thought I was in the right place?

"Counsel, you're an 'uptown' lawyer," the magistrate continued with air quotes, "and this criminal docket is most decidedly 'downtown.'"

That got a collective chuckle from the assorted lawyers who were still benched and waiting for their own cases to be called.

Ah, now I got it.

Earlier, when I entered the courtroom, I'd signed in, as all lawyers were required to do, listing my client's name and mine, along with name of the law firm I was with. Big Law was not, to put it mildly, a habitué of the drugs-and-murder docket. Seeing Dunn & Sullivan on my sign-in sheet, this judge was about to have some fun with me.

"We don't see you guys in here all that often. So what gives, Counsel? Slumming?"

Trick question, of course. I said nothing, simply smiled as pleasantly as I could and hunched my shoulders in a *Beats me, Judge*, pantomime, all the while mentally stacking sandbags against my flooding thoughts of grand juries and criminal charges.

The magistrate was just getting some kicks at my expense, ineligible as he and the lawyers in here were for Big Law membership. That door was permanently locked so far as they were concerned. (If only they knew.) This magistrate—a forty-something, olive-toned, middle-aged guy with a hairline so low there was hardly any forehead showing—would get in another jab or two, and then he'd get back to business and arraign my client.

So that was not going to be a big problem here. The big problem was that I was keeping the fact of my representation of Señor Alvarez from my law firm.

I had not, as required by firm rules, opened a new client file. Nor would I. No way would Dunn & Sullivan allow me this representation in the firm's name, even if I weren't doing this for free. That was so even if I were to tell them that I was doing it to save my brother's life. And no, I also hadn't notified the firm that I was also acting as counsel to my brother in *his* criminal case.

"I guess all those stories we've been reading about the hard times you ivory-tower lawyers are having are true. You being here and all."

I went for another bemused shoulder hunch. After waiting for something more from me and not getting it, the magistrate finally turned to his bailiff and told him to begin the arraignment.

"The defendant will rise," the bailiff told the already-standing Geraldo. Then harshly demanded to know how the defendant pleaded to the ten or so crimes he'd been accused of committing.

"Not guilty," Geraldo told the guy, no doubt thinking something like, *You and me? You fat fuck. Anyplace other than here? You talk to me like that? I skin you alive.*

The not-guilty plea now on the record, the magistrate turned to the prosecutor.

"What's the bail situation?" he asked.

The federal prosecutor hadn't so much as glanced my way. She was very young, seemingly fresh out of law school, just north of albino white with frizzy, colorless, center-parted hair and elongated Freddy Krueger fingers. She would continue ignoring me for the scum-sucking, low-life criminal-defense lawyer she considered me to be, Dunn & Sullivan partner or not.

"The government opposes bail," she said. Then, pointing an accusing skeletal forefinger over at Geraldo, she added, "This defendant is a danger to the community."

"Over to you, Counsel," the magistrate told me.

And so I made my argument for bail based on what Geraldo had told me when I'd visited with him in lockup earlier in the day. He was a naturalized U.S. citizen and had no prior convictions. Yeah, okay, he'd had twelve or so arrests.

All but one set of charges had been dropped when witnesses had either had a change of heart about what they saw and knew or had died before trial in a variety of ways (run over by a car, shot in the back of the head while waiting for a bus, etc., etc.). His one and only prior trial resulted in an acquittal on all charges. His mother living with him was the necessary ties-to-the-community part of my argument.

When I finished, the prosecutor slowly read off a list of names, pausing for dramatic effect after each one.

Juan Ortiz

Jamie Acosta

Consuelo Suarez

And so on.

When she finally got to the last one, she told the magistrate those were the names of witnesses against the defendant in prior cases, each and every one of whom had either come down with terminal amnesia or died under suspicious circumstances before they could give testimony.

"This man, Your Honor," she repeated, "is a danger to the community."

The magistrate looked back over to me.

"Counsel," he said. "Under the Bail Reform Act, do I not have the power to deny someone bail if I determine he is a danger to the community?"

"You do, Your Honor," I said. "But unsupported allegations from the prosecutor"—here I did glance over at her and smile as coldly as possible—"are not sufficient. There needs to be more before you can make such a finding."

The magistrate turned to the prosecutor.

"Counsel, what say you?" he asked her.

"Your Honor, the government has given you more than enough information for you to deny bail."

(Translation: that was all she had.)

We stood waiting as the magistrate made up his mind.

Then he threw me a bone, maybe because of the good-natured way I took his ribbing. More likely because I had made the better argument.

"The court will set bail in this case at five million dollars. The defendant is ordered to surrender his passport and the U.S. Marshals are instructed to provide an electronic ankle bracelet that the defendant is to wear at all times. It is further ordered that the defendant will be confined to his home and may not leave said premises unless and until he gets permission from this court, which permission will not be freely given."

The magistrate then turned his attention to Geraldo, who had just given me a little hip bump, pleased as he was with the court's decision. A five-million-dollar bond would be issued by a bail-bonding company upon the payment by Geraldo of a 10-percent premium. The 10 percent for Geraldo, five hundred thousand in cold, hard cash? No problema.

"Mr. Alvarez," the magistrate said. "Do you understand these conditions?"

"Yeah."

This time a hip bump from me.

"Yes, Your Honor," Geraldo quickly added.

"Will you abide by them?"

"Yes, Your Honor."

"Next case," the magistrate then said as the marshals took Geraldo away for processing and release once bail was posted. The prosecutor and I left the well of the court, still without a word between us.

I left the courtroom, walked down the hall, and took the elevator back down to the lobby and security, where I'd had to leave my cell phone as the rules of this court required. I handed the chit I'd been given earlier back to the guard, who then searched the wall of cubbies for the matching number and my phone. Once it and I were reunited, I took the revolving doors out to Pearl Street and powered up my cell.

As I waited for it to return to life, I must say I felt a sense of accomplishment. I know that sounds weird given the dangerous person I'd just helped to gain some temporary freedom, a guy who was undeniably a threat to the community. But that's the system. Better ten guilty go free than one innocent unjustly convicted. The presumption of innocence. All of that. The prosecutor hadn't done her job. I had done mine. That's what I was paid to do. Okay, not in this case, but that's not the point. I had lawyered. And lawyered well.

My phone lit up and pinged. There was a voice-mail message waiting. The number on my screen was the main number for Dunn & Sullivan. I tapped LISTEN and listened.

The message was from Carl Smith's secretary. It told me that I was to go to Mr. Smith's office immediately upon hearing this message. I called her and gave her my ETA, then flagged a cab. Riding uptown, I silently replayed the scene in the courtroom.

Once back at Times Square, I entered our building, quickly dropped off my papers in my office, and headed for Carl's.

"Mr. Smith and Ms. Stankowski are in there waiting for you," the secretary told me.

Anka? In there? Had the firm learned I hadn't opened a new client file? Was that it? Couldn't be, not yet. Then what?

The minute I walked in and saw their faces, I knew.

48.

"Sit down."

Carl pointed to one of the two chairs at the foot of his desk.

As I took the seat, I got a glimpse of Anka seated to the side over in the sofa-and-chairs portion of Carl's office. Once I was seated, she would be out of my line of sight. She could see me—and Carl—but I couldn't see her. Instinctively, I smiled at her before sitting down. She didn't return it. Just stared.

"This is going to be very difficult for me," Carl said, his demeanor consistent with that being nowhere near the case. He was speaking for the record, his words carefully chosen so they could be repeated more or less verbatim at some later point. (Which in fact they were.)

"I don't know what you're talking about," I told Smith.

(Though I did.)

"Of course you do," he said with a quick glance over at Anka.

I was about to turn my head back to Anka when Carl continued.

"The FBI has been here, did you know that?"

"What?"

"Come on, Blake, don't act so stupid."

To say I was uncomfortable was an understatement. What could I say? Or do?

"Okay, Blake. I'll lay it out for you," Carl added after an uncomfortable silence.

And he did, informing me that Dipak Singh, whom he described as *my* "colleague and foreign co-counsel," had been arrested in India and charged with making illegal payments to the judge down there. It seems the judge had also been arrested and charged with corruption and graft. And Carl was telling me that I had discovered all the nasty shenanigans those two had engaged in and had run with the case anyway, making me an integral part of the criminal conspiracy to pervert justice.

Despite his assurances, Peter Moss did sell Dipak out after all. There had been a regime change in Dipak's state, and the new government was much friendlier with worldwide conglomerates like GRE. Dipak and his family had lost their clout. That made him, and them, dead meat. And so to try to save his own skin, Dipak had given some visiting FBI agents a sworn statement implicating me with knowledge and participation in his criminal conduct.

No sooner had Carl finished, "That's bullshit, and you know it," I said.

Carl said nothing. His look said everything.

And what the hell was Anka doing here? And why wasn't she coming to my defense?

Why?

Because Anka had been collaborating with Carl Smith all along, ever since I'd first approached her.

Carl had been using her to egg me on to keep the GRE case alive so it would remain on Dunn & Sullivan's books as a major law-firm asset. She was the one slated to receive that big slice of extra stock (remember the blank stock-transfer agreement?) when the IPO went live. That was to be her payment for assisting Carl.

"Blake," Carl said, "you are a bad apple. Dunn & Sullivan does not tolerate bad apples. You are hereby dismissed from this law firm."

There was nothing more to say. I was about to get up when there was a knock on Carl's door.

The three of us turned to see Smith's secretary stick her head through the open crack.

"They're here," she said. And then stepped aside as three guys in dark suits walked in.

"Carney Blake," one of them said.

"Yes."

"I'm Special Agent Steven Daley. And I have a warrant for your arrest."

The secretary had no doubt called them as instructed by Smith when I'd phoned in from downtown with my ETA.

Still seated, I watched as Special Agent Daley pulled a copy of my arrest warrant from his suit jacket and displayed it to me. Then he told me to stand up, turn around, and put my hands behind my back. I did as told, and he handcuffed me.

"Is this really necessary?" I asked, if not in actual shock, more or less stunned.

Agent Daley ignored my question.

"You have the right to remain silent," he told me instead. "You also have the right to an attorney. If you cannot afford an attorney, one will be appointed. . . ."

The agents led me out of Carl's office. As we passed the secretary's outer desk, I heard her on the phone.

"No, I'm sorry, Mr. Moss," she said to the caller. "Mr. Smith is indisposed right now and will have to call you back."

What?

The FBI agents perp-walked me down the hall to the elevator

bank. A thousand eyes were on me. Into the elevator we went, then down to the lobby and out to the sidewalk, where a small phalanx of reporters and camera crews were waiting.

I was led through them as they shouted questions my way. There was a black Chevy Tahoe at the curb. I was led there and guided onto the backseat.

As I looked through the side window, I could see a collection of microphones held in the direction of Carl Smith, who must have come down here on the next available elevator. With Anka at his side, he was making what was obviously a statement about my arrest and Dunn & Sullivan's helpful assistance to the authorities.

Then the Tahoe left the curb, and with lights flashing I was driven to the Manhattan Correctional Center and a waiting jail cell.

And that was that.

TWO YEARS
LATER

49.

Sean and I passed through security.

We had returned from Cahill's Bar to the federal courthouse on Pearl Street after I'd gotten the call from my lawyer that the jury had reached a verdict. We walked through the metal detector, surrendered our cells as required, and then rode the elevator back up to the courtroom on the fifth floor.

We were the first to arrive. Sean and I took seats on the front bench just outside the rail. I could feel the anticipation of the jury's verdict even though the courtroom was still empty. It electrified the air. Not long after, the judge's bailiff entered by a side door and began setting things up. He had brought in some files that he placed on the judge's bench, refilled the judge's water glass from a silver pitcher, and so on.

He ignored us.

Then the lawyers started coming in. The two Assistant United States Attorneys who had prosecuted the case took their seats at the government's table. A smattering of federal agents who had assisted them grabbed seats on the first-row bench across the aisle from Sean and me. One of them nodded to me. It was FBI Special Agent Steve Daley, the guy who had cuffed me and read me my rights in Carl Smith's office. I nodded back. Then my lawyers came into the courtroom.

It had not been easy finding counsel. Several of the lawyers I approached had begged off. It was one thing to defend a lawyer accused of fraud and another to defend a lawyer accused of fraud when the defense was that an irreproachable powerhouse law firm like Dunn & Sullivan had set the lawyer up. Making the law firm the bad guy in a case like this was considered an unhelpful career move, one that could result in a slow professional death.

My lawyer did a better job than I thought he would have. Why? Because of Jeremy Lichtman.

Soon after my indictment and arrest, Jeremy quit the firm. So did Gloria Delarosa. By then I had been released on my own recognizance. We three met at my apartment.

"Unnecessary," I told Jeremy.

He waved me away dismissively.

"Stay at that place without you?" Jeremy said. "Under circumstances like these? No fucking way."

And Gloria? Well, she was part of the team. A good soldier. If the team moved, she moved with the team. I saw the way Jeremy looked at her as she told me that she, too, had quit. The guy was really in love. (It never went anywhere, not that Jeremy ever gave up trying.)

The three of us set up shop. The bar hadn't yet disciplined me. The disbarment proceeding was held in abeyance pending the outcome of my criminal trial. That meant I could hold on to my license to practice in the interim period. But what law firm was going to hire me? So we started our own little firm. And thus was Blake and Lichtman born.

We had two clients. Me being the first.

Jeremy entered my criminal case as co–defense counsel. By pre-trial motion the judge had ruled that Jeremy could act as co-counsel even though he had previously been employed at Dunn & Sullivan. The prosecutors, thinking Jeremy was just some wet-behind-the-ears kid lawyer not long out of law school, told the judge they had no objection. They obviously believed that having an inexperienced, bumbling young advocate on our side would, if anything, help their side score an easy conviction.

You won't be surprised to learn that as the case progressed, Jeremy (with Gloria's paralegal help) carried more than his share of the load. He wound up doing some of the most important cross-examination, and he made one of the best final arguments to the jury that I think I will ever hear.

Our second client?

Geraldo Alvarez.

So Geraldo had watched the tape of my arrest that afternoon two years ago on Time Warner Cable News (NY1) on the TV bolted up on the wall outside the holding tank. He decided not to post bail for himself immediately. That way he could remain in the holding cell when I got there and protect me from the other inmates in case I needed it.

"Hey," he told me as we sat side by side on one of the cell's long benches. "Ain't this some shit, you and me in here together?"

Yeah, great.

I was released, and then Geraldo posted his bail. Unfortunately, not three days later he was rearrested on witness-intimidation charges, and this time he was held without bail. He also started paying us fees. I guess he took pity on us, since he was our law firm's only outside client.

I heard the whoosh of the courtroom entrance doors swing open and turned around. My dad and Diane were there. Not together. You can be sure of that. Seamus's racial-tolerance needle remained stuck, as it was, on zero. No, they only arrived at the same time, probably were on the same elevator up to the fifth floor. They ignored each other, yet each knew who the other was. (They'd both been at Rosy's burial.)

My father had been in this courtroom every day of the trial.

I had moved back to the Hell's Kitchen apartment while Sean was upstate at a rehab facility as part of his "one bite of the apple" plea deal. My dad's bladder cancer seemed stable enough. Still, Sean and I felt he really should have someone at home with him. He did go to his periodic outpatient treatments, but—surprise, surprise—he wouldn't quit drinking. To give him his due, though, he had cut back some.

The prosecutors had offered my lawyer a plea deal. Also called a plea bargain. This was some bargain.

I had to plead guilty to one of the four felony counts in the indictment that charged me with fraud and obstructing justice in my handling of the GRE case. If I did, the prosecution would then make a nonbinding recommendation to the judge for one year in prison. "Nonbinding" meant that the judge was perfectly free to ignore this recommendation and throw the sentencing book at me. (Each count could land me in prison for up to five years, for a total of twenty, if I was convicted on all four of them. And, needless to say, I could kiss my law license good-bye.)

My lawyer urged me to take the deal, told me that juries hate lawyer defendants, especially lawyer defendants like me, who had so much and still broke the law to get even more. (Apparently he didn't buy my insistence on innocence.) He said it was my best shot.

Since I was living at the Hell's Kitchen apartment back then, sleeping in my old room, I told my dad about the deal offer. We were sitting at the dining-room table where that disastrous Thanksgiving dinner had taken place a couple of years earlier.

"Did you do it, boy?" he asked as he sipped his Jameson's from a juice glass.

"No, Dad," I said. "I didn't."

"Then tell those bloody bastards to take that deal and shove it up their arses."

And that, more or less, is what I did.

As I've said, Seamus was in here on one of the benches every day that court was in session. Was he drunk? A little. But he never made a scene, didn't speak to anyone. He was just there for me, his son.

I watched my father wait to see where Diane was going to sit, and then he sat elsewhere. Diane and I exchanged smiles. She herself had spent her days prosecuting cases in the nearby state courthouse and so hadn't seen much of the trial. But she called me every night to let me know she was there for me, no matter what.

Jeremy and my lead lawyer and Gloria came through the swinging entrance doors and walked down the aisle to their own counsel table. Jeremy motioned for me to join them, and I did.

Then the bailiff reentered the courtroom.

"All rise," he announced. "Oyez! Oyez! Oyez! The United States District Court for the Southern District of New York is back in session, the Honorable Michael Fetterman presiding. God save the United States and this honorable court."

Once reseated, I watched the judge look over first to the prosecution's table and then ours.

"Counsel," the judge said, "we have a note from the jury. They have reached a verdict. Shall we bring them in?"

"Yes, Your Honor," both sides said.

"Very well," the judge said, then told the bailiff to do just that.

I watched as the bailiff knocked on the side door at the opposite end of the courtroom. He opened the door and stepped aside as the jury members one by one filed back into the jury box.

There's another old trial lawyers' adage: If the returning jury looks at the defendant, that's a good sign. If they don't, it's curtains. You're going down.

I sat at trial table between my two lawyers, intently watching the incoming jurors.

One or two took a quick glance in my direction. Most seemed purposively to look away.

Oh, boy.

50.

They say your life flashes before your eyes when you're about to die.

It's supposed to be some sort of chemical phenomenon where a massive dose of adrenaline is released into your system and in literally seconds all that you were and all that you did sprints across your mind's screen.

The jury members were still taking their seats. Everyone in the courtroom sat perfectly quiet. Waiting. Tension rode the air like a hot current. It's always like that when a jury returns with a verdict.

I wasn't dying, though it felt like it. Somehow the days of testimony that had preceded this very moment shot through my head like a bullet. (Shades of Mad Dog.) It jolted me.

Dipak Singh had been the first prosecution witness.

Part of his plea deal in India was the obligation to appear at my trial in New York. On direct examination he testified that I knew all about his payoffs to the Indian judge, that he had disclosed everything to me at our London luncheon. He claimed that I'd sent Jeremy away from the table, so he wasn't there when Dipak spilled the beans.

Jeremy didn't cross-examine Dipak, since he was part of the London luncheon scenario. (He also didn't testify that Dipak was lying about his absence from the table. You can't ordinarily be a witness and a lawyer in the same case.) My "lead" lawyer did only a so-so job. He tried to get Dipak to admit that he had taken money under the table from Peter Moss to bring Dunn & Sullivan into the case.

The payoff funds were well hidden by a wire transfer from an offshore account to an account under a fictitious name in India. So Dipak denied it even though the paper trail, such as it was, showed timing consistent with such payments.

"No, my good sir," Dipak had said. "I have not received anything from this man . . . Peter Moss. Never even met the gentleman."

I saw juror number seven nod. Was he buying Dipak's perjury?

When it was her turn on the stand, Anka Stankowski told the jury that she had done her best to supervise me and had repeatedly asked for assurances that all was on the up-and-up.

"I was very careful with this young man," she testified on direct examination, after trying her best to squeeze her voluminous frame into the narrow witness chair. "With hindsight I can say that something seemed not right, but he kept assuring me that all was in order. You know our firm enjoys the highest reputation, and I did my best to see that this young partner behaved properly, as both our law firm and the law itself demands."

On cross-examination Jeremy confronted Anka with documents we had subpoenaed from Dunn & Sullivan showing the big bump in stock she was to get once the IPO took place.

She acknowledged the extra stock but claimed it was merely an incentive for the time she spent monitoring young partners like me. And anyway, she told the jury, there hadn't been an IPO, so she got nothing. (With my indictment, the impending trial, and the attendant bad publicity, Carl and the bankers had decided to let things cool off before pulling the trigger on the IPO.)

Another nod from juror number seven, and now one from juror number two.

And then firm chairman Carl Smith took the stand.

I have to admit, he gave a masterful performance on direct examination. He was charming, removing his eyeglasses from time to time and addressing his responses to the jury as though they were cherished friends.

Carl told the jury how saddened he was about the rotten apple he'd had to pluck from the golden barrel that was Dunn & Sullivan. Such a tragedy, he said, shaking his head in grief for the benefit of the jury. Such a promising young man. Yes, maybe he should have pressed harder about what was going on in the GRE case. But he had sought and received repeated assurances from me that all was going smoothly, as he had from Anka, to whom he had delegated the task of keeping tabs on me.

"We value our reputation," he told the jurors, eyeballing each one in turn. "Still, I can't help feeling sorry for this young man. If it were in my power to forgive him, I would," he added, making clear to the jury that they need do no such thing.

On cross-examination Jeremy did his best. He later told me how weird it felt at first, cross-examining his former law firm's chairman, but how quickly that hesitancy dissipated and how he had no trouble going after the son of a bitch.

The trial transcript bears it out.

Jeremy: Carney Blake wasn't the only young partner to whom you assigned one of your law firm's contingent-fee plaintiffs' cases, isn't that right?

Carl: As firm chairman I don't assign cases. Others do that for me.

Jeremy: So you are denying under oath that you had any role in assigning those cases to young and relatively inexperienced partners?

Carl: I didn't say that. You're twisting my words.

Jeremy: It is a fact, is it not, that you had a role in selecting Carney Blake for the GRE case?

Carl: (*doing his best to wiggle out of the question*) Are you asking me to explain our law firm's case selection procedures?

Jeremy: No, sir, I am not. (*then . . .*) I will ask the court stenographer to read my last question back to you.

Whereupon the stenographer read back Jeremy's last question verbatim.

Jeremy: (*continuing*) Do you understand the question? Yes or no.

Carl: (*glowering at Jeremy—did the jurors see that?*) Yes, I understand the question.

Jeremy: Then answer it.

Carl: Yes.

Jeremy: Yes what?

Carl: (*visibly annoyed*) Yes, I had a role.

And that's pretty much how it went. Carl admitted that all of the contingent-fee cases Dunn & Sullivan took in had been assigned to young and relatively inexperienced partners. He also acknowledged that Big Law typically did not take on these kinds of cases. Carl affirmed the IPO plan, but like Anka he blew it off because there had not been an IPO (yet).

Jeremy hammered at Carl for another hour or so. Now, unlike during his behavior on direct, Carl was visibly testy with Jeremy as he was continuously confronted with questions he didn't like. That surprised me. I didn't think Carl would lose his cool like that. Jeremy had gotten under his skin, no doubt about it.

Carl was the last prosecution witness. The government then rested its case. Following a motion by the defense for summary dismissal of all charges (quickly denied by the judge), it was our turn.

We had some accounting experts and legal scholars testify about plaintiffs' cases and how Big Law had historically acted as defense counsel and not plaintiffs' lawyers. We tried to put a banking expert on the stand to testify about this new quest for law-firm IPOs and the windfall profits they would generate for certain partners. The prosecution objected, telling the judge that this had no relevance to what I did or didn't do. The judge bought it and wouldn't allow our evidence.

I did not take the stand in my own defense.

I wanted to. Thought the jury needed to hear from me. My lawyers (Jeremy especially) said no. Too risky, they said. If I took the stand, on cross-examination I would have to admit that I didn't catch on in time to all the bad shit that was happening. And I should have. Or the jury wouldn't buy my explanation and conclude that I was lying, that I must have figured out what was going on and chose to do nothing about it. Either way I would look bad in the eyes of the jury. So no. Don't take the stand, they said.

It was my call.

I listened to my lawyers and didn't testify. If that was a mistake, it was a big one.

Then we rested.

Both sides made final argument, the judge instructed the jury what law to apply to the facts, and the jury members were then sent back to their room to deliberate.

And we waited. It took the jury three full days to reach a verdict. As I said earlier, at one point during the second day, the jury sent a note out to the judge telling him they were hopelessly deadlocked and couldn't agree on a verdict.

The judge ordered the jury back into the courtroom and read them the Allen or dynamite charge, and then sent them back for more deliberations. On day three they reached a verdict. And now here they sat as the judge addressed their foreman.

"Mr. Foreman," the judge asked, "has the jury reached a verdict in the case of the *United States versus Carney Blake?*"

The foreman rose to his feet. "We have, Your Honor."

"Have you completed the jury verdict form you were handed when you began deliberations?"

"We have, Your Honor."

The judge then instructed his bailiff to retrieve the completed form and hand it up to him.

I sat between my lawyers and watched as the bailiff retrieved the form and walked it over to the judge's bench. The judge unfolded the paper and read it. He looked at me.

Hard as I tried, I couldn't read the judge. His face was absolutely blank. I quickly glanced over to the jurors. The foreman had retaken his seat. Not one juror was looking my way.

"Prepare yourself," my lawyer whispered as the judge handed the form to the bailiff with instructions to return it to the jury foreman. I turned for a quick glance at the spectators' gallery. My brother, my dad, Diane—all of them were intently watching me. I tried a weak smile but couldn't even manage that. I turned back to face the front of the courtroom.

Jeremy and I exchanged glances. Was that worry I was seeing? Of course it was. How could it not be?

The courtroom was still. Not a sound.

"The defendant will rise," the judge said.

I got to my feet.

"The jury foreman will rise," the judge said.

He got to his feet.

The judge nodded to the bailiff.

"How say you?" the bailiff asked the foreman. "As to count one of the indictment. Is the defendant Carney Blake guilty or not guilty?"

The foreman looked down at the sheet of paper between his hands. He said nothing at first, seemed to be . . . what? Rereading it? Did he catch a mistake? What was taking him so long?

Then he looked up. He faced the judge. He faced the prosecutors. Then us. But he wasn't really looking at anything. He seemed frightened? Worried?

And then.

The bailiff, repeating. "How say you, Mr. Foreman? As to count one of the indictment. Is the defendant Carney Blake guilty or not guilty?"

Jeremy got to his feet and stood beside me. That caused my other lawyer hesitantly to do the same. Jeremy gripped my arm and held tight.

"As to count one," the foreman finally said. "We the jury find the defendant Carney Blake . . ."

ANOTHER TWO
YEARS LATER

EPILOGUE

"Mr. Blake?"

I rise to address the judge. "Your Honor?"

"Are you ready to give the jury your opening statement?"

"I am, Your Honor."

"Then kindly step to the podium, and let's get this show on the road."

This judge is like that, using vernacular phrases ("show on the road"), thinking it makes him appear less stuffy, more a man of the people. This anemic-looking Asian-American jurist, sporting an early Beatles mop-top haircut and granny glasses, who had been appointed by a very conservative president, thinking the judge was a safe-bet right-winger, and whose views then did a one-eighty once he was confirmed by the Senate. So what? His views are his business, as long as he runs his courtroom fairly and efficiently. As he does.

I grab my notes and slowly walk to the podium set up directly in front of the jury.

As you no doubt have figured out by now, I was acquitted on all charges. It was torture standing and waiting for the bailiff and the foreman to work their way through all four of the counts in the indictment. I think I held my breath so long that I almost passed out by the time the foreman announced the final "Not guilty."

And a lot has happened since then.

Peter Moss's Mason Rose and Dunn & Sullivan merged. Well, they called it a merger, but it was more an acquisition, a semi-hostile takeover by Peter Moss's law firm of a crippled Dunn & Sullivan, and most decidedly not a merger of equals.

Big Law was still spiraling downward. Defections continued, as did loss of revenue. Peter Moss had brought his corporate-raider skills to the game. At the now-combined law firm, he quickly cleaned house, firing even more deadwood lawyers and staff. He dumped those other worthless plaintiffs' class-action cases that Carl had brought in. Ruthlessly stole as many clients from competing law firms as he could. Moss brought "New Law" to what had been Big Law.

Before the merger—in fact, soon after my arrest and indictment—Carl had withdrawn Dunn & Sullivan's legal representation of the Indian plaintiffs in the GRE case. (Moss then dropped his lawsuit against the firm and me.) The newly minted law firm of Blake and Lichtman picked up the case.

We dismissed the New York lawsuit seeking to seize GRE's assets based on the Indian court's judgment and filed a different case back in federal court in Manhattan to try the entire matter anew. By that point there was no reason not to do so. Most all of what had happened earlier was by then on the public record. We established jurisdiction to keep the case in court and overcame all delay issues raised against us.

By then the takeover of Dunn & Sullivan had been completed. The combined firm was renamed Moss and Sullivan.

Moss and Sullivan wanted to continue the GRE defense begun by its predecessor, Mason Rose, subject to any objection from us. I told the judge we had no objection. *No problema*, as Geraldo Alvarez would have said.

And speaking of Geraldo.

His case did come to trial, and he was acquitted. It seemed that the wiretap had not been lawfully authorized, and so almost all of the prosecution's evidence against him became inadmissible.

"Nice going," Geraldo told me after he was released from custody. "Thanks, Counselor."

"You're welcome."

"And I didn't have to kill anyone this time. Much easier."

"Tell me you're joking?"

Geraldo didn't respond. He shrugged his shoulders. Whatever.

He's back in jail again, held without bail on a new set of charges Blake and Lichtman are still his lawyers. In fact, thanks to the earlier acquittal, we've picked up a growing roster of criminal cases. Between that work and the plaintiffs' civil cases we now handle—almost all opposing Big Law firms, all on percentage-of-recovery fee arrangements—our firm's revenue has steadily climbed.

But that's not the primary reason we take on those new civil cases. Nope, it's the sheer pleasure we get out of beating the pants off Big Law. (And we don't use hedge funds to finance our cases. We hold back a portion of our fees and keep them in a war chest to fund subsequent ones.)

I'm standing at the podium adjusting my notes. About to begin my opening statement to the jury. I look up and smile at them.

My memoir was published several months after my acquittal. My publisher was eager to get the book into the shops and onto e-readers while my story was still fresh. One of the jury-qualification questions posed by GRE's defense counsel—none other than Mr. Peter Moss in the flesh—had the judge ask prospective jurors if they had read my book. I agreed that any prospective juror who had actually read the book would be excused from service.

This case being the civil suit about to commence by the Indian plaintiffs' class against GRE.

And where was Carl Smith in all this?

After the "merger" he and Peter Moss served as co–managing partners of the reconstituted law firm. Guess how long that lasted? Peter Moss still had it in for Carl. There would be no forgiving and forgetting. Like the Italians say, revenge is a dish best served cold.

Carl finally took his hand off the coconut when he withdrew Dunn & Sullivan's representation of the GRE plaintiffs, as I said, pre-merger, at the time I was arrested and charged.

And what does he do? He sticks his hand right back through the hole in the box. It seems there was another coconut in there all along. And this one was even bigger. Even juicier. That other coconut? The IPO, of course. And there was Carl's fist, now grasping that other coconut for dear life.

Carl still wanted to cash out. The problem was that Peter Moss wanted to cash *in*. Big money was to be made from a revamped version of traditional Big Law. The last thing Peter Moss needed was independent outside stockholders looking over his shoulder. So, as far as he was concerned, there would be no IPO.

Carl pushed and pushed. He had reinvigorated the bankers. That wasn't hard. Bankers were like the carriage horses tourists take from Columbus Circle for a spin through Central Park. They both wore blinders when it came to doing their jobs.

So Carl pushed, and Peter Moss then pried Carl's tight fist off that second coconut. How did he do that?

Carl was expelled from the new firm.

The grounds for said expulsion? It starts with the NYPD.

About six months after Polly's untimely death, the cops finally got around to questioning William Cunningham. (The wheels of justice do grind slowly.)

Our young bodybuilder was forced to acknowledge that he had indeed been in Polly's apartment on the fateful day of her death and that his hands had for a time been wrapped around her neck. (He had denied all until the cops showed him the fingerprint, DNA, and security-photo evidence.) But kill her? Actually cause her death? Absolutely not, he'd told them in teary, gasping sentences. He had also admitted that Carl Smith and he had been lovers at the time and that it was at Carl's direction that he'd paid his threatening visit to Polly at her place.

Then, as so often happens, nothing happened.

Before the statute of limitations could run, however, William was finally charged with attempted murder. Long before then he and Carl had called it quits.

Well, *Carl* had called it quits, thinking that if it came to it, he would claim he was so aghast at what William had done up there in that East Side apartment that he'd ended his amorous relationship with this young, misguided fellow. In fact, he had prepared a contemporary memo to his eyes-only personal file at the time of Polly's tragic death, just to be sure that his real feelings and convictions would be preserved for the police, should they ever need them. In sum, Carl finally admitted his little homosexual dalliance, figuring it wasn't the big deal these days that he had considered it earlier to be.

It wasn't, but the article written by a certain perennially disheveled young female correspondent, formerly with the *New York Law Journal* but of late on the reportorial staff of—yes, you guessed it— the *New York Times*, really did Carl in.

Julia Grossman's gratitude to Peter Moss for having gotten her the interview that got her the job was robust. (He told her how bad he'd felt standing her up, as he had, despite the urgency of the situation.) She didn't let Peter actually draft her story about Carl's sneaky and amoral behavior (married as Carl was at the time) but willingly included Peter's narrative, if not word for word then close enough to make the story really sting.

Carl looked bad, not necessarily because of what William had done but for the manner in which Carl had conducted himself both before and at the time of Polly's death. And (surprise, surprise) Iván the Impaler had secretly kept a second set of images of Carl and William's Florida poolside performance. The *Times*, of course, would never actually publish such photos, but Julia gave them prominent mention in that part of her story describing Carl's messy divorce proceedings before they were terminated by Polly's death.

Under those circumstances how could Moss and Sullivan possibly keep this senior partner on?

Carl has retained excellent criminal-defense counsel and, at the time of this writing, has not as yet been indicted as an accessory to attempted murder.

So . . . back to the GRE case.

Several days ago, on the eve of trial, Moss called me.

Me: What's up?

Him: You're gonna lose your case. You know that, don't you?

Me: You called to tell me that?

Him: I read your book.

Me: (*waiting*)

Him: (*continuing*) Reads like a novel.

Me: Ah, you're calling as a literary critic.

Him: Well, no. As it so happens, I have a settlement offer for you.

Me: You do?

Him: It's good only until the trial starts. Then it's withdrawn. Understood?

Me: Understood.

Him: Ten million.

Me: Declined. Thanks for calling.

Him: You're making a big—

I hung up.

Then, after the jury was empaneled and just before court began this morning Moss upped his offer to $25 million. I huddled out in the hallway with my team.

My team?

Jeremy and Gloria, of course. But Diane and Sean also.

Diane had left the DA's office and was now practicing law with us. I think that will work out just fine, even though we're engaged to be married. And Sean? He's off drugs, though he's still drinking too much, but he's working for Blake and Lichtman. As what? Good question. I'm really not sure, but it seems to be grounding him, and the others are okay with the arrangement.

And while he's still back at the office and not out here in the hall with us, remember that big African guy from the lockup? He's clean now, too. I think. Anyway, at Sean's urging he was hired as our reception-ist. We needed to buy a bigger desk to fit him behind. But no matter.

Huddled in a circle, I asked my team should we take the offer.

Thumbs-down all around.

So here I am at the podium, about to begin. I look back over to the judge. *Now?* I signal.

Now, he signals.

But first I take a quick peek over to the spectators' gallery. I see my dad sitting in the last row. He looks bad. Probably going to die soon. We lock eyes. *Go get 'em, boy*, he's silently telling me.

And then I turn my attention to Peter Moss, who is sitting at the defendant's table with two of his young partners. I'm facing away from the jury.

Remember my first in-court session with Moss? His infuriating wink out of the jury's view?

Since *my* back is to the jury, they can't see my face. I wait until I get Moss's full attention. Our eyes lock. I give him the sweetest smile, like, *Isn't this fun?* Just a couple of colleagues at the bar having a good old time. And then I wink. Moss glares at me. Perfect. The jury couldn't have missed that. I turn to the waiting jurors.

"Ladies and gentlemen of the jury," I begin, my face set in the most solemn of expressions.

"You are about to hear a story of depravity. A story about the depths that the defendant GRE, a big, fat worldwide conglomerate, will sink to when it comes to protecting its riches at the expense of the lives and safety of its day-to-day workers. And when this story is over and all the evidence is in, I will come back up here and make final argument. And when I get back up here, I will ask you to return a verdict for the plaintiffs in this case in the amount of one billion dollars."

And know what?

When the case ended, the jury did just that.

ACKNOWLEDGMENTS

Gratefully, I find myself once again in the capable hands of my publisher, David Rosenthal. And once again I am amazed by his insight and skill. We've worked on several books together over the years and he has remained not only a valued colleague, but a good friend as well. I can't thank him enough.

Thanks also to my copyeditor, Maureen Sugden, who did a thorough job of understanding my story and characters and ensuring that nothing got lost along the way as she performed the nitty-gritty art of reviewing and considering the efficacy of each word, every punctuation mark, and so on.

David's expert assistant editor, Katie Zaborsky, was enormously helpful each and every time I called on her, even when, by any standard, my question(s) could be considered less than brilliant. Thank you.

Marilyn Abraham, who had a successful career in publishing, edited my first novel, *Grand Jury*. Throughout the years we have remained friends. She and her husband, former publishing executive Sandy MacGregor, have provided a steady source of critical reading of my work. Their feedback has been invaluable.

ACKNOWLEDGMENTS

Throughout my years as a practicing lawyer I was fortunate to be surrounded by, and on occasion facing off against, some of the country's best lawyers. I also spent many years as a player in the docudrama called "the practice of law." From my federal judicial clerkship, to the U.S. Attorney's office, to a boutique law firm, to my twenty-seven years in Big Law, I had an interesting and fascinating journey, involving some great inspirational material. Thanks to you all for giving me so much to write about.

And finally, my love and thanks to my best friend, loyal reader, and wife, Simma; to our daughters, Shana and Margot; and their husbands, Michael and Aaron, for their love and support. And the mere thought of our four grandchildren is so joyous that it provides all the fuel needed to fill my creative tank.

ABOUT THE AUTHOR

Ron Liebman has been a law clerk to a federal judge, an assistant United States Attorney, partner in a boutique litigation law firm, and a senior partner in one of America's top law firms. He is the author of three novels, *Grand Jury, Death by Rodrigo,* and *Jersey Law,* and editor of and contributor to the nonfiction *Shark Tales: True (and Amazing) Stories from America's Lawyers.* Ron lives in Washington, D.C., and Easton, Maryland, with his wife, Simma Liebman. Their two daughters and their families live in New York.